ISABELLE DAY

REFUSES TO DIE OF A BROKEN HEART

With best
wishes —
Jane St. Anthony

**ALSO BY JANE ST. ANTHONY
PUBLISHED BY THE
UNIVERSITY OF MINNESOTA PRESS**

Grace Above All

The Summer Sherman Loved Me

Isabelle Day

REFUSES TO DIE
OF A BROKEN

HEART

JANE ST. ANTHONY

University of Minnesota Press

Minneapolis · London

Published by the University of Minnesota Press
111 Third Avenue South, Suite 290
Minneapolis, MN 55401–2520
http://www.upress.umn.edu

Design and production by Mighty Media, Inc.
Interior and text design by Chris Long

Library of Congress Cataloging-in-Publication Data
St. Anthony, Jane.
Isabelle Day refuses to die of a broken heart / Jane St. Anthony.
ISBN 978-0-8166-9799-1 (hc)
ISBN 978-0-8166-9922-3 (pb)
1. Grief—Fiction. 2. Friendship—Fiction. 3. Minnesota—History—20th century—Fiction.
I. Title. PZ7.S14131S 2015
[Fic]—dc22   2015013269

Printed in the United States of America on acid-free paper
The University of Minnesota is an equal-opportunity educator and employer.
20 19 18 17 16 15   10 9 8 7 6 5 4 3 2 1

For Emily and Edward—
supportive, creative, loving, and loved

CONTENTS

1
UNHAPPY HALLOWEEN

Isabelle Day locked eyes with a malevolent jack-o'-lantern. The pumpkin, refusing to blink, stared at her from the house across Barrett Avenue. Isabelle dropped her gaze from the window and turned, looking back into the living room of the upper duplex.

She wouldn't be trick-or-treating tonight. Who would she trick-or-treat with? Mom? She felt as hollow as a pumpkin without pulp. Last year even pumpkin slime was funny. Dad had made himself a mustache with it.

"You want the front bedroom, don't you?" said Isabelle's mother, hidden behind cardboard boxes in the dining room. "That's what you said, isn't it? I can't seem to remember anything." The lilt in her voice was forced.

"Fine," said Isabelle. It didn't matter.

She watched the movers carry the frame of Mom's new twin bed. Although Mom had brought almost none of Dad's personal belongings, nearly every item bore his imprint: the couch where they sat to watch baseball games, the dining room table for Sunday dinners, the stereo cabinet with the record player that sparked Dad and Mom's impromptu dances.

"Take that bed to the back room, please," Mom said, pointing.

When the movers emerged, cigarettes wobbling between their lips, they headed for the stairs and another load. A bit of ash floated down to the living room carpet. Isabelle and Mom saw it at the same time. Isabelle waited. Mom didn't say a word to the movers.

Isabelle turned back to the window. She couldn't avoid Mom in this half-house. At least she could climb through her bedroom window and sit on the front porch. In the summer, it might almost be a tree house. No one would see that she was alone.

"Here's your dollhouse," Mom called, as if Isabelle were cataloging her childhood possessions. "Front bedroom," she said to the movers.

The dollhouse looked out of place, a rosebush in the desert. Isabelle turned back to the window. The houses across the street had one mail slot in the door or a mailbox at the front of the house, not two as the duplex did. There were no brick houses. Stucco prevailed. Most were smaller than the houses in Isabelle's Milwaukee neighborhood but substantial enough for families.

"That dresser goes in the front bedroom, too," Mom said to the movers. She stood at the window with Isabelle and watched a woman push a baby carriage on the sidewalk. The woman stopped for the parade of dining room chairs, then strolled as she inspected the items piled on the boulevard.

"You would think she'd never seen a moving van before," said Mom with a sigh.

Two little girls on a porch across the street caught Isabelle's attention. Each wore a jacket zipped up to her chin. They held their dolls facing outward as if to show them the activity across the street. The girls' four pigtails appeared to be at the same height. Twins?

"About the moving van," Isabelle said, because the silence was thick. "We never saw one unless somebody died." She sucked her breath in and wished that she had considered her words before they flew out. Mom pressed her lips together tightly. "I'm sorry," said Isabelle.

Mom looked as if her lips were sewn together while her eyes did the talking. The sight of Mom acting brave made Isabelle want to wail. But it was true about the moving van. Until the past spring, no one

Isabelle knew had left this world except for Grandma Olive and Mr. Butler, their neighbor, who died in bed with his hand in the popcorn bowl while the television blared. "I think he met his maker before *The Tonight Show* was over," elderly Mrs. Schumacher speculated. A moving van had arrived for the furniture that Mrs. Butler brought to her son's house with her.

Isabelle's spacious three-story house in Milwaukee was made of brick. When she learned to print her name, Isabelle wrote it in chalk on the back of the house, one letter per brick—and added chalk flowers. After adorning eight bricks, Isabelle found Dad in the basement and asked him to come outside.

"That's amazing," he said, his admiration apparent. "Extraordinary." He paused. "Chalk is a good choice, honey. But if you decide to write a book on these bricks, don't use paint. Your mother would turn us into a couple of scrub brushes."

After a while, Isabelle's name faded. Rain helped. Now Milwaukee would fade, too.

Isabelle went to the kitchen for a glass of water.

"Do you need anything?" Mom said, without looking at Isabelle. She lifted a dotted swiss kitchen curtain from a box.

"No, I'm fine."

Mom tried to fluff the curtain, but it rebelled, reverting to its flattened state. "It will take a while to settle in, but this is the neighborhood—well, close to it at least—that I grew up in, and you'll love it, too. Someday."

"Sure." Who was Mom talking to? Love it? A duplex in a strange city with no dad and no friends and a couple of invisible landladies creeping around below?

Isabelle took the water back to the front window. A skimpy handful of yellow leaves clung to the birch tree in the front yard. The branches frantically scratched the porch railing as if they had a message for Isabelle. The pumpkin glared.

2
DON'T MESS WITH THE SPIRITS

At a few minutes past five o'clock, Isabelle surveyed the neighborhood from the open porch that ran the length of her bedroom and the living room. Pumpkins, now lit with candles, leered back. A slow parade of the youngest trick-or-treaters moved up and down the block in the dusk.

High heels tapped the sidewalk, muffled briefly on the crunchy leaves, and Mom came into view, climbing the steps as Isabelle looked down on her. The front door of the duplex opened and shut.

Isabelle climbed in through her window. She walked through the bedroom that seemed to be someone else's in spite of her nubby bedspread and fuzzy rug and bookshelf and dresser with the statue of the Virgin Mary on it. Last Halloween her candy had almost covered the bedspread. What a torture

Halloween was when you stayed inside. Who cared if she was an eighth-grader? Carol and their friends were trick-or-treating tonight in Milwaukee.

"I'm back with the Almond Joys," Mom called from the living room.

"Okay," Isabelle said. She slipped into a cardigan and opened the door. "Here I go." Mom handed the bags of candy to her, and Isabelle trudged down the steps.

A mixing bowl with individually wrapped popcorn balls sat on a little table in the hallway, courtesy of the two landladies. Mom had met them—the McCarthy sisters—earlier in the day. "They're dears," she reported.

Isabelle stared at the popcorn balls nestled in red cellophane. They were tempting. Would anyone hear her unwrap one?

"Little Girl," called a high-pitched voice behind the first-floor door.

Isabelle jumped, her heart booming.

"Little Girl, let the children help themselves, won't you? My sister and I can't get out of our chairs quickly enough. Can you hear me?"

"She can unless she's had her eardrums surgically removed," said a second, lower voice behind the door.

A wave of dread washed over Isabelle. Life was complicated enough without two crones asking her questions or pinching her arm to see if she was plump enough to push into the oven for dinner.

"Dora, shush, dear. You'll scare her before she's even met us."

"Then maybe she'll stop thundering on the stairs like a herd of elephants on its way to a peanut farm."

"Oh, Dora, how you make me laugh!"

"It's true, Flora."

"I can hear you," Isabelle said in a voice louder than she meant it to be.

"Help yourself, won't you, Little Girl?" said the first voice, which must be Flora's.

"Yes, I'll help myself." Was this her new life? Talking to doors?

"All is well, then. We'll meet you on another day that's not quite so trying as Halloween. Oh, the corn syrup we went through!"

"And for what?" said the other voice, Dora's.

"Good-bye," Isabelle said, to signal the end of her participation. In the future she would tread softly when she went in and out. Little Girl. Not good.

The doorbells to the upstairs and the downstairs rang in quick succession. Isabelle turned from the McCarthys' door and opened the outer door for the first group of trick-or-treaters.

"There's no one upstairs," she said. "Everything is here."

"Are you a mom or a kid?" asked a hobo at the front of the group. His mouth moved in a face spotted with ash, fake dirt. A tree branch hung over his shoulder, and a knotted pillowcase of allegedly earthly possessions swung at the end of it.

"Neither," said Isabelle, dropping candy and popcorn balls into the open bags. Why did he think she was a mom? Was it because she was wearing Mom's lipstick and tossing candy into bags? "I'm a witch. I've been dead for three hundred years."

The hobo scowled. "You're creepy," he said.

"You're dirty," she replied, releasing Almond Joys and popcorn balls into the bags of a sheeted ghost and a cowgirl.

The hobo glared. "Moms don't talk that way to kids they don't know."

"I told you. I'm not a mom. I'm a witch."

"Sicko," the hobo said.

"Hobos should stick to the rails. And you forgot to say 'thank you' for what I dropped in your dirty pack."

"Right." The hobo backed away—his posse already heading down the sidewalk. He tripped and stumbled without falling.

"I did that to you," Isabelle called after him. "Next time, don't mess with the spirits." She sat on the bottom step and waited for the next batch of kids whose masks scared each other silly.

At eight thirty, the foot traffic was over, and Isabelle flipped off the porch light and climbed the stairs. Mom sat paging through a math book at the dining room table. Her job as a long-term substitute teacher at the closest public elementary school would begin tomorrow. One of the fifth-grade teachers had returned to North Dakota to care for her ailing mother.

"Big turnout?" Mom asked. "I heard a lot of little voices."

"Not like home."

"Are you going to share the leftovers with me?"

"You can have them. I'm going to bed."

"I'll leave the extra key on the kitchen table in the morning," Mom said as Isabelle walked away. "And the phone number so that you can leave a message for me in the school office if you need anything."

"Right." Mom had told her this multiple times.

As Isabelle headed for her room, she remembered what she hadn't done. She dutifully returned to the dining room. "Good night," she said, bowing her head for Mom to plant a kiss on the part in her hair. This was the worst time of the day. The clinging style of hug must be avoided so that she and Mom wouldn't dissolve in tears.

Seated on her bedroom floor, Isabelle inspected the items in one of the cardboard boxes: the bride doll that Grandma had let her pick out, the jewelry box with the broken clasp, her piggy banks, the clock radio. She put the radio back into the box. She wouldn't need it tomorrow. Catholic school kids were released from school on the day after Halloween, All Saints' Day.

She picked up the black-and-white framed picture of Dad with his arm around her in front of their house on the first day of kindergarten. She and Dad were almost the same height because he was kneeling on one knee next to her. After placing the photograph on the dresser, she picked up the one of her and Mom in the same pose. There hadn't been an extra person to photograph all three of them. Maybe it was a warning: someday, you, Isabelle, will have your entire family in one frame, the frame with you and Mom. She put the photograph next to the one with Dad.

Isabelle scavenged in one of her boxes until she found *Anne of Green Gables*. Two nights ago she had read on a blanket on the floor, the last night in her true bedroom. Last night she had slept on the couch at the home of Cindy, Mom's old friend, while her life in boxes was en route to Minneapolis. Tonight she read the same page twice yet couldn't remember what she had read. Isabelle pulled the lamp chain and, in darkness, listened to the branches scrape the porch. From the kitchen she heard the noise that was more upsetting than any sound she had ever heard: Mom's soft, gulpy sobs. Isabelle pulled the pillow over her head. How could she comfort Mom? She couldn't comfort herself.

3
LANDLADY ALERT

Rain streaked the windows. It was a perfect day for staying inside—as if she had anyplace to go, Isabelle thought. She slept until Mom called on her lunch break.

"Is everything all right?" Mom asked. A typewriter rattled in the background.

"I haven't used my voice yet. How are the kids?" Talking to Mom on the phone was easier than talking in person.

"This is hard to believe, but two of them have parents I knew in school."

"Do they look like their parents?"

"One does. Timmy Staples. I think I have a crush on him."

Isabelle made a face. "That is so gross."

"It's even more odd because it's his mother he

looks like. Isabelle, leave a note for me if you go out, okay?"

"Okay." Isabelle felt locked in someone else's house.

"I'll see you after three thirty," Mom said.

"Right." Isabelle breathed in Mom's absence. She didn't feel happy, just lighter. Mom doubled the sorrow in any room.

As soon as she replaced the phone receiver in its cradle, Isabelle heard footsteps on the front stairs. At least Mom had ordered the phone to be hooked up yesterday. She could call the police if someone tried to break in. Isabelle stared as if she might be able to see through the door.

Silence hung there. Someone must be listening on the other side. Isabelle put her hand on the phone.

"Little Girl?" called a very old voice, the voice that belonged to the giggling McCarthy sister, Flora. "Are you at home, dear?"

Should she pretend she wasn't? The voice must know that she was there or she wouldn't have traveled upstairs.

The McCarthy sisters might be an enormous burden, asking her to play canasta or visit on Saturday night or watch *The Guiding Light* with them when she was home from school. Even though she didn't have friends here, she would rather not spend time with centenarians.

Isabelle addressed the door. "I have a terrible stomachache, so I'm going back to bed." She made her voice shaky. "I'm probably contagious. Maybe it would be better if I met you another time."

With no response forthcoming, Isabelle continued, "It hurts to move." She groaned for dramatic effect.

The pause on the other side of the door persisted as seconds ticked by on the clock in the dining room. The clock had belonged to Dad's grandfather, so Dad called it the grandfather's grandfather clock. Had it always been this loud?

"I'll leave some chicken soup at your door, Little Girl. I'll rap to let you know when it's here. Open the door when you can." The soft padding of feet melted away.

After Flora McCarthy left, Isabelle plugged in the television that sat in a corner of the living room. She flipped through the channels, keeping the volume low. The feature on Mel's Movie Matinee was *Letter from an Unknown Woman*, which she had seen on television with Carol in Milwaukee. It was the saddest movie she had ever watched. But somehow, it didn't seem as sad this time. During the second commercial, Isabelle coated saltines with peanut butter. Leaving the movie on for company, she dressed and began unpacking her records and books and sorting them in the bedroom, moving as quietly as possible.

The rain stopped and the wind picked up,

threatening to fling pieces of gray sky around like roof shingles. Isabelle took cover in bed and began to read, planning to appear active when she heard Mom on the stairs.

She fell asleep reading.

"What's this bowl of soup doing on the top step, Isabelle?" Mom called as she entered the living room.

Isabelle rolled over in bed and saw her open book on the floor. As the wind continued its tantrum, Isabelle tried to recall where she was. She looked around the room and remembered, her stomach sinking. "One of those downstairs people must have brought it for me because I told her that I had a stomachache so she'd leave," she said, wondering if the McCarthy sisters could hear her words clearly. She didn't want them hovering, but it was pointless to hurt their feelings.

Mom stood in the open doorway. "So you met her?"

"We talked through the door."

"Why didn't you eat this for lunch?" Mom said, walking to Isabelle's room as she raised the bowl to her nose. "It smells so good. Like chicken soup should smell."

"I fell asleep." There was no use pretending that she had put her room in order. "She must have knocked lightly."

Mom put the bowl on top of a box and hung her raincoat in the closet. "It's nice to walk, even in this weather," she said, rubbing her temple with two fingers as if she could dissolve a headache. "I made so many decisions so quickly. Wouldn't it make more sense for us to go to the same school?"

Isabelle didn't answer. Why would it matter where she went when she didn't know even one person at either school?

Mom walked to the kitchen and returned with two spoons. "Want to share?" she asked, picking up the bowl of soup before lowering herself into the rocking chair.

Mom was a sparrow, Isabelle thought, a pretty little sparrow. She had lost weight, although she hadn't had much to spare. People said that they could be sisters, although Isabelle had passed Mom in height and had less delicate features. Her brown eyes were Dad's—"hungry puppy eyes," he had called them.

"I don't want any soup," Isabelle said. "And I don't care where I go to school."

Mom rocked slowly, not responding. She tried to act as if their lives were normal. Today she had stood in front of Timmy Staples and other kids she didn't know and pretended that everything was fine.

"How was school?" Isabelle asked, to make sure that Mom hadn't given up talking.

"Oh, fine."

Mom kept rocking. Dad was gone, forever. That was not fine.

4
WALKING TO BEDLAM

Isabelle combed her hair as she looked in the full-length mirror propped against one wall of her room. After she told her best friend, Carol, that she was moving, Carol had given her a headband. Now she lowered it onto her head. The smooth reddish-brown plastic was embedded with stars, tiny and gold. Isabelle tried to avoid seeing herself below the neck. Her uniform jumper, a brown V from shoulder to waist that connected to a limp skirt, was light-years beyond ugly.

"I have to leave, Isabelle," said Mom.

Isabelle cracked open her bedroom door. "I'll leave when I find a big box with a neck hole. Maybe I should switch schools so I don't have to wear this thing."

Mom peered in. "It's not so bad. You're pretty no matter what you're wearing."

"It makes my old uniform look like a prom dress."

"You'll be in the same boat as everyone else."

"Not consoling."

Mom wore a dress of green-and-blue plaid with a modestly scooped neck set off by a white collar with little scallops. A belt cinched her waist. Her shiny hair bobbed on her shoulders when she moved.

"You're a Breck girl," Dad used to say, referring to the serene, smooth-haired shampoo models. "When they look for a Breck boy, I'm here."

Dad's hair had a life of its own. Before he brushed it in the morning and even after, it was a thick, clumpy dark tangle, each hair having a different destination. Isabelle had tried wetting her hair or setting it on big rollers, but it always sprang back. Although she had complained about her hair, she was pleased to resemble Dad in any way.

"See you after school," said Mom, shutting the door softly.

Isabelle ate a bowl of Kix and wished that she hadn't. The contents of her stomach sloshed around as if trying to escape. She sat for a few seconds until the storm quieted a little, calming herself by imagining that she could walk past the school. No one would recognize her, so she could keep walking until she made a plan. She slipped into her jacket and locked the front door behind her. She padded down the stairs and past the McCarthys' entrance as quietly as possible. The sisters might be lurking, ears pressed to the door, poised to creep out and waylay her with a stale popcorn ball.

Isabelle walked to the corner of Barrett Avenue and crossed it, moving on Thirty-eighth Street toward the church steeple that pointed heavenward in the pale sky. She scanned the park on her right, noting the baseball diamond, tennis courts, sprawling park building, and swings and slide and monkey bars. The park seemed to go on forever, like the distance to school that stretched out like a gauntlet.

"It's the witch!" a voice called as Isabelle passed the first alley. A boy in tweed pants and a hooded jacket looked sickeningly familiar, like a character in a bad dream.

"You're the witch across the street," he said, emerging from the alley. His hobo face was scrubbed clean.

"I thought I told you to hit the rails," Isabelle said. "Why are you here?"

"Probably going to the same place you're going, unless you wear that uniform because you like it. Sixth grade," the boy said, pointing to his chest.

"Eighth," said Isabelle, not pointing.

"My sister is in eighth grade," said the boy, falling in step with Isabelle. "Her name is Margaret."

"Where is she?"

"She already left. It's her week to hang up the smart kids' papers and stuff."

"Is she in nun training?" Isabelle tried to keep

her voice light but realized how sarcastic she must sound. The boy didn't seem to notice.

"No, everybody in her room takes a turn."

When Isabelle couldn't think of anything to say, the boy said, "I'm Mark."

"Isabelle."

"What room are you in?"

"316."

"That's my sister's room," Mark said. "Three eighth-grade rooms, and you're in hers."

"Is the teacher good or bad?"

"Margaret says she's the worst."

"Oh, great."

They walked the rest of the way without talking, except when Mark pointed out neighborhood landmarks.

"Paint store on Lyndale. The family lives in back."

"Interesting."

"That's the public school." It spanned a city block. "Agassiz."

"I know. My mom teaches there."

Mark didn't respond. Moms didn't go to work.

They kept walking. "Dairy Queen," said Mark. A giant soft-serve cone on the sign confirmed it. "Barnett's," he said, gesturing toward the drugstore across the street.

It was better to walk with a hobo than alone, even if he was someone's pesky little brother.

"The babies go there," Mark said, looking across

the street as they neared the intersection with the church, convent, and two school buildings, each on its own corner. "Sixth, seventh, and eighth grades, this building."

"I know. My mom and I registered on Halloween."

Mark stayed with Isabelle as she climbed the stairs to the third floor. She didn't say thanks because she thought she might lose control if she opened her mouth. Had she ever done anything harder than stand in front of this classroom door? She flashed on the last time she had seen Dad. Yes, she had done something harder. She had found her father, minutes after he had died. She braced herself.

The noise hit Isabelle as soon as she stepped through the door that opened into the back of the room. Kids in uniforms sat on desktops, talking and laughing. By an open window, a boy gestured with a lit cigarette in hand. How could they get away with this? Was it some kind of unsupervised jail for juveniles?

Suddenly a lookout in the hall jerked the room's front door open, his raised hand apparently signaling an alarm. A hush descended. The cigarette flew out the window. An invisible magnet pulled everyone into his or her seat. Anarchy reverted to order.

Sister Mary Mercy roared into Room 316. Although her feet gripped the floor, her anger hurtled ahead of her. She sniffed the air.

"Out, Charles Hager! Out for defiling our room!"

she commanded in a voice coated with ice. "Remove your rusty fingertips from our presence and proceed to the office where punishment will be meted out!"

Charles swaggered out the door at the back of the room. He was taller than Sister, who smiled demonically as if imagining his inquisition with the principal.

Sister Mary Mercy's dramatic outrage, Charles's smirk, and the kids' obvious delight in the production convinced Isabelle that this was not the first cigarette that Charles had enjoyed in the classroom.

"As for the rest of you," Sister said, taking in the remaining fifty-one eighth-graders, "what kind of inferno must our new student believe that she has entered?" She narrowed her eyes at Isabelle, who remained by the back door. "All of the tormented souls engulfed by hell's fire could not compete with the ungodly noise from this classroom."

Sister glared at her students for a few seconds, then turned to Isabelle. "And now," she said, "we welcome you to Room 316. Kindly introduce yourself."

"Now?" Isabelle croaked. The bell rang.

"At the front of the room and, yes, now." Sister made a sweeping gesture with her arm, intended to give Isabelle the floor. "If you will," she added in a slightly warmer tone.

Isabelle moved forward. Every step was labored.

"My name is Isabelle Day," she said, looking at the blur of faces. To calm herself, she focused for a moment on the picture at the back of the room.

St. Sebastian, the first Christian martyr, hung there, his body riddled with arrows.

"I was born in Milwaukee," she continued, not sure how much information Sister expected. St. Sebastian appeared to be bleeding profusely. "I moved here on Halloween. My mother is a teacher at Agassiz."

"What is your favorite subject, Isabelle?" Sister asked.

Isabelle fumbled for an answer. Reading was her favorite subject, but should she stand here and divulge her life story? It wasn't anyone's business—including Sister's. "History," she said. But not mine.

"Excellent!" Sister pulled her hands from behind the long swath of scapular that hung over the front of her habit like a table runner. "Now please take the seat at the back of the room."

Isabelle's skirt brushed against the desks on either side of the narrow aisle. Her corduroy jacket didn't protect her from the stares. This is what a leper must feel like, Isabel thought. She had suffered through Bible-based references to the dreaded disease almost every year since third grade. Now she felt as shunned as if she carried *Mycobacterium leprae.* She slid into the only empty desk chair.

"You need to hang up your jacket," said the girl whose desk was across the aisle from Isabelle's.

"No talking!" boomed Sister. "It's time for morning prayers."

The girl raised her hand. "May I show her the cloakroom, Sister?"

"Well, then. Take her."

The girl stood. Isabelle followed her to the folding doors, which the girl opened so that Isabelle could hang her jacket on a hook. "I think that you live across the street from me," the girl whispered, her back to Sister. "I'm Margaret, your neighbor."

"You live with the hobo."

For a second, Margaret paused. "My brother on Halloween, right?"

"Right." Isabelle connected the dots. "Are those little girls your sisters?"

Margaret nodded, shut the cloakroom doors gently, took her seat, and smiled at Isabelle.

Isabelle sat across the aisle, grateful that Margaret didn't detect any leprous nodules or deformities on her. But no matter how kind Margaret looked, Isabelle did not want a neighbor. She wanted a friend, preferably an old friend from Milwaukee.

5

BENEATH THE SILVER TRAY

At lunchtime Isabelle followed Margaret down the staircase. A girl from their room with a strawberry blond ponytail waited on the sidewalk.

"Are you going home for lunch?" Margaret asked Isabelle.

"I think I have to. I'm only seven blocks from school."

"That's right," said the girl with the ponytail who was now walking with them. "You have to live at least eight blocks away to get lunch at school."

"This is Grace," Margaret said to Isabelle.

"Hi," said Isabelle.

"Welcome to the zoo," Grace said. "Room 316, I mean."

Isabelle began to walk, and Margaret and Grace stayed with her. Margaret was a little taller than Isabelle, with shiny brown hair and a calm face with searching green eyes. Grace had freckles and strands of red and gold hair that escaped from her ponytail. She looked wound up, coiled, a dramatic kind of girl whose face seemed to have more expressions than most faces.

"Now you know two people in our class," said Margaret.

Isabelle nodded. *Knew* them?

"Do you have sisters or brothers who go to school here?" Margaret asked.

"No."

"Well, you have a mom and dad."

"Just a mom." Isabelle felt Margaret and Grace's embarrassed silence.

"Where's your dad?" Grace asked as they passed the drugstore.

Where was Dad? Isabelle felt herself caving inward.

"Dead."

No one said anything. They walked, looking ahead.

"Your mom and dad were your whole family," Margaret said quietly, almost to herself. "I'm sorry."

Isabelle wished that she could tell Dad about this awful day. She bit the inside of her cheek to keep the tears from starting. If she spoke, her voice would crack.

A group of girls skirted around them, two on each side, without a break in their conversation. Isabelle watched them re-form, in step, words streaming like liquid as they walked.

"Let's have lunch at your house," Margaret said to Isabelle. "Then you'll have company."

Isabelle nodded.

"I don't mean to invite myself over, but it would be fun to go to your house. If you came to my house, the twins wouldn't leave you alone."

"Those little girls with pigtails are twins?" This was good. She was talking. No one was asking her questions about Dad.

"They would cling to you like leeches," Grace said. "They think they're one person so they really like company."

"Would your mom mind if I came over?" Margaret said.

"I don't think so."

"I have to turn off here," said Grace.

"Do you want to come over, too?" Isabelle asked.

"I have to make everybody's lunch at my house. Don't forget to pick me up on your way back."

The crowd of kids walking home thinned out.

"Do you always walk to school and back from school with Grace?" said Isabelle.

"Unless one of us is sick. But now we can walk together and meet Grace at her corner."

Did Margaret feel sorry for her? Was she this nice to everyone?

As they approached the duplex, Isabelle whispered

to Margaret to step lightly. The girls smelled something before Isabelle unlocked the upstairs door.

"Who cooks your lunch when no one is here?" Margaret asked. She followed Isabelle through the living room and dining room and into the kitchen.

"The landladies downstairs, I think," Isabelle said as she gazed at the tray on the table. A silver dome covered a large plate. Were meals included with rent? Impossible. People sent mountains of food to Mom after Dad was gone. But those people knew them.

"What is it?" Margaret asked.

Isabelle lifted the cover slowly, revealing the floral pattern on the plate's rim. Steam rose from a lumberjack's portion of thinly sliced roast beef, mashed potatoes that encircled a lake of gravy, and cooked rutabaga.

"Everything but a wine goblet," Margaret said. "I bet that's dessert under there."

Isabelle plucked the red-and-white checked towel from a pie plate. An apple pie pushed steam through the juicy slits in the top crust.

"I can't imagine what they would bring for dinner," said Margaret. "How did they get in? Or know when you'd be home?"

"They're landladies, so they have a key. And they must have asked my mom when I'd be home for lunch."

"They're nice," Margaret said. "They brought

dinner to us when the twins were born. They even watch a twin once in a while. Have you met them?"

"They talked through the door at me on Halloween and the day after."

"It's not their fault they're so old. I don't think they have much to do."

Both girls jumped at the rap on the back door. Isabelle walked to it and looked through the window, where she saw the top of a small head with white hair. She opened the door.

"Oh, Margaret," said Miss Flora, looking past Isabelle and addressing the girl she knew. "I want to make sure that Little Girl sees what we brought for her while her mother is at work."

"That's her."

"Oh, yes, of course. How do you do, dear? I hope that I'm not intruding, but my sister, Dora, and I wanted you to have a nice hot lunch on your first day of school. Is it still hot?"

"Very hot," Isabelle said. Miss Flora didn't look like a predatory crone. She was a lovely dried flower with a knot of white hair at the back of her head and a floral bib apron trimmed with rickrack.

"That's good. I am delighted to meet you. Goodbye to you, too, Margaret. Say hello to your mother for me. Are those little twins behaving?"

"No, they hardly ever behave."

"Margaret, you're teasing me. They're such precious little ones." Miss Flora paused. "Let me run downstairs and get lunch for you, too."

"There's more than enough for both of us," said Isabelle.

"If you're sure. Good-bye then, girls." She turned to begin her descent.

"It's hard to imagine her running downstairs," Isabelle said after the footsteps had faded. She took two forks from the silverware drawer.

"I forgot to call my mom," said Margaret. "Where's the phone?"

Isabelle pointed to the wall. She tried not to listen as Margaret talked to her mother. It sounded like normal mother-daughter talk, rapid conversation that flowed easily and with no words left unsaid lurking under the surface.

As Isabelle spooned mashed potatoes onto her plate, she wondered if Miss Flora was a typical landlady.

"This is the best roast beef I've ever had," Margaret said. "You need a cleaver to cut what we eat at our house."

The beef was tender and the gravy rich. Isabelle wanted to tell Margaret that she, Isabelle, had two things that she hadn't had in the morning: an unexpected hot lunch and, maybe, a girl across the street who might want to be her friend. But she pushed away the idea. She didn't want to appear as desperate as she felt.

6
SEA OF DOILIES

Isabelle rang the doorbell inside Margaret's porch on Friday after school. Mark, Margaret's hobo brother, answered the door.

"Is Margaret home?" Isabelle said.

"I guess so. She just walked home with you."

Isabelle sized him up: a lot of swagger but not mean.

"Would you tell her that I'm here?"

"I heard that Miss Flora and Miss Dora are making your lunches now."

"That was one day."

"Just once?"

"Does Margaret even live here?"

"Margaret!" Mark yelled without turning away from Isabelle.

Instead of Margaret, two identical girls in red

cardigan sweaters skipped into the living room and stood next to Mark.

"Hello," Isabelle said.

"Are you a princess?" one of the girls said.

"She's a witch," said Mark.

"No, she's a princess," the first twin said to the other.

"A princess?" Isabelle looked down at her corduroy pants to see what the twins saw.

"You're wearing a crown," the first twin said. "Like a princess."

Isabelle felt her head for a crown and touched her headband from Carol. "Oh," she said, "the stars."

Margaret appeared in the doorframe between the dining room and a hallway. "Hi," she said, walking toward Isabelle.

"I need you," Isabelle said over the heads of Margaret's siblings. "My mom saw Miss Dora hauling stuff up from the basement and told her I'd help. Do you want to help me?"

"Right now?"

"She wants it in the garage so that it's ready for the trash collection on Monday or next year or something. So, yes."

Margaret retreated to wherever she had come from earlier. Isabelle heard voices but couldn't decipher the words. Then Margaret sailed through the dining room and past Mark and the twins and Isabelle to the front hall closet where she slipped into a jacket.

"Do you live in a castle?" one of the twins asked Isabelle, who couldn't remember which twin had spoken first.

"The castle dungeon."

"A dungeon?" the twin said to the other twin.

"It's a place where people are sent to be unhappy," Isabelle said. "They can't ever escape."

The twins looked at Margaret. "Escape?" one of them asked.

"You don't want to start something with them," said Margaret to Isabelle as she walked toward her. "They never run out of steam."

"We love you," said a twin. "You're pretty." The other twin nodded solemnly.

On a Saturday morning in the spring, Isabelle, Mom, and Dad had sat in their bathrobes, each reading a section of the newspaper as they finished the soft-boiled eggs prepared by Mom and the potatoes that Dad had fried with onions. Sunlight spilled onto the kitchen table, hinting at a day full of possibilities.

"I feel great," Dad said. During the last winter, he had stayed in bed for days in a row.

He lowered the newspaper and looked over his reading glasses at Isabelle. "You must be the prettiest girl in the seventh grade," he said. "What's the matter with me? The prettiest girl in Milwaukee. No, anywhere."

"You're just saying that because I have your hair," said Isabelle, beaming. "You love it on me."

"Your mother must have contributed something to your good looks," Dad said. "An eyelash?"

Mom laughed and a few drops of yolk escaped her mouth indelicately.

In the last pictures Dad had taken of Isabelle, she looked like a giraffe wearing a clown's wig.

"You'll be a beautiful woman," Mom had said when they looked at the pictures. Even though she meant her words as a compliment, they upset Isabelle. Dad never said that she had to wait to be beautiful.

Now Mark lifted his hand in parting, which snapped Isabelle out of her reverie. Was the hobo being nice? Isabelle waved her fingers back. He had walked her to Room 316 after all. It would have been horrible to climb the steps alone.

"Good-bye, girls," she said to the twins.

"I am Kathleen," one twin said. The other stared.

Outside, the wind teased the brown grass. "I can't believe you didn't wear a jacket," said Margaret. "My dad said that it was twenty-six degrees outside when he got up."

"I bet it's less than twenty seconds, door to door." Isabelle ran across the street, Margaret closing in on her as they neared the front porch.

"It's open! Come in!" called Miss Flora when Isabelle knocked, and the girls stepped into the living room. Miss Flora's smile shone as brightly as the lamplight on her hair.

The McCarthys' living room looked as if a sea of doilies had washed through, leaving a memento on every surface. Each doily, it seemed, was topped by a framed photograph of a child or children in old-fashioned clothes. The curtains were rectangular doilies, as was the tablecloth on the dining room table. The sofa and chairs—arms topped with doilies—looked plump enough to swallow Miss Flora. An ancient phonograph stood on a small table in one corner. The combined scent of apple and cinnamon filled the air.

"Margaret, how nice that you came to help our dear Little Girl," Miss Flora said. "You girls take the apple crisp out of the oven and put some in the dishes on the table. After we eat, we'll help Dora. She doesn't want any crisp."

"Shouldn't we help you in the basement first?" Isabelle said.

"The work will wait, dear. Let's talk a little before we hurry downstairs."

They settled in the dining room where a pot of marigolds bloomed by the south windows. Isabelle looked across the table at Margaret and said, "Miss Flora has a daughter named Margaret." Mom would be proud of her for remembering this.

"Right," said Margaret.

"She lives across the river in St. Paul, so I don't see her as often as I'd like," Miss Flora said.

"Doesn't she come over almost every Sunday with

the kids?" Margaret asked. "Or pick you up and take you to her house?"

"You are correct, Margaret. But it would be lovely if she lived close by."

St. Paul was across the river, Isabelle knew. How many seconds away could that be?

"Margaret is my youngest daughter," Miss Flora said to Isabelle. "Someday I'll tell you about my other babies." She took a handkerchief from the sleeve of her buttoned-up sweater and dabbed her eyes with it. "There, I'm better now." She blew on a spoonful of apple crisp.

Isabelle and Margaret exchanged looks.

"Miss Flora," said Margaret, clearing her throat twice before continuing. "Why is your name 'McCarthy'—like your sister's—if you were married?"

"Well, dear, after my husband passed on and I moved to this duplex with Dora—we certainly didn't need the big house anymore—we started calling ourselves the McCarthy sisters again, just for fun. And that was fine with me because my husband's last name was—let's just say that it was difficult for some people to pronounce."

"What was it?" said Isabelle.

"Zakresevski," Miss Flora said. "Try saying that quickly ten times!"

"I couldn't say it once," said Isabelle.

"Ditto," Margaret said.

"You girls are such comedians! Of course you could say it, if it were yours. And yet, it seemed easier to use our given name, McCarthy." She sat up straighter in her chair.

"Radical," said Isabelle.

"Think of us as movie stars," Miss Flora said.

Movie stars? Isabelle repeated in her mind. The grandfather clock's tick-tocking underscored the silence.

"Some of them made up their names," continued Miss Flora, mercifully. "Judy Garland was born Frances Gumm. But some of the stars kept the names given by their parents, like Olivia de Havilland and Katharine Hepburn."

Isabelle shot a look at Margaret. Was this accurate?

Mom's footsteps sounded overhead.

"We should get downstairs before your sister does all the work," Isabelle said. She scraped the sides of the china bowl with her spoon.

"You'll have to come back for a real visit soon," said Miss Flora. She rose by bracing herself on the table.

Isabelle and Margaret followed Miss Flora to the kitchen, where they put their bowls in the sink.

"Many hands make light work!" Miss Flora said as she opened the door that led to the basement.

"This is the most fun I've ever had," Margaret mouthed to Isabelle.

Isabelle gave her a soft punch to the upper arm. What she couldn't say was this: I'm so happy that you're here with me and that I'm not upstairs where Mom is tiptoeing around the emptiness.

7
BREAKFAST HOSTAGE

Isabelle woke up on Saturday to a silent duplex and remembered that Mom had bused downtown to do errands. With the family reduced to two, Saturday morning breakfasts had ended in Milwaukee.

After acting as the McCarthys' mules the previous evening, Isabelle and Margaret had gone to Margaret's house for fish sticks and *The Twilight Zone*. Isabelle wanted to melt into Margaret's family. The house reverberated with cheerful noise.

Frost laced the windowpanes. Isabelle wrapped herself in a wool blanket and went to the kitchen to make toast. Should she call Margaret after she ate or wait to see if Margaret called her?

Someone tapped at the door. Margaret?

"Dear, are you in there?" called Miss Flora.

Isabelle's stomach took a dive. We have to move

immediately, that's what she would tell Mom. Miss Flora might be a nice person to grow moldy with in Doily Land if you were about one century old. Otherwise, no thank you.

"I'm here," Isabelle said, trailing the blanket into the living room.

"May I see you, please?" Miss Flora said. "The door seems to be in the way."

What would it be this time? Moving the trash back inside?

Miss Flora stood one step below Isabelle. She smoothed her potted geranium apron. "Oh, Little Girl," she said. "My sister and I want to thank you for helping us last night."

"It wasn't a big deal."

"We're going to give you a proper breakfast. You haven't had breakfast, have you? We saw your mother leave."

Isabelle lifted one foot from the cold floor, balancing like a flamingo. "Did you invite Margaret, too?" Margaret had hauled as many bags of junk as she had.

"Yes, I called her, but she was helping her mother with the cleaning."

Isabelle imagined keeping a bowl of excuses next to the door. "I have to finish my history project." *Shut the door.* "The toilet just overflowed." *Shut the door.* "I'm allergic to doilies." *Fake sneeze and shut the door.*

"Dear, I know that you rush out of here on school

days, but we can't rest knowing that you're upstairs on a Saturday morning pouring a bowl of cold who knows what. Now get your bathrobe. My sister will be worried that something terrible has happened if we take all morning."

This time, she would go. But never again would she answer the door.

In her robe and slippers, Isabelle padded down the stairs after Miss Flora. The only sturdy thing about the landlady was her pair of black lace-up shoes with thick, wide heels, seemingly the only type of shoe sold to grandmotherly women.

"I found her," Miss Flora trilled to her sister from the living room.

Isabelle followed her to the kitchen that faintly held the apple-cinnamon fragrance of the previous day.

Grim as roadkill, Miss Dora stood at the stove surrounded by the grinning cherries, pineapples, and bananas in the wallpaper. She was the slightly heartier sister, able to lift boxes in the basement and, now, scoop what looked like a trough of steaming oatmeal into a bowl, which she handed to Isabelle.

"That might be too much," said Isabelle, taking a seat.

"You look as if you could blow away in a breeze, child." She stood over Isabelle's shoulder and cut a large pat of butter from a butter dish and plopped it on top of the oatmeal, added brown sugar, and poured cream from a white pitcher over all.

Miss Dora's tiny amethyst in a gold band sparkled.

"That's a pretty ring," Isabelle said, surprising herself by saying it out loud.

Miss Dora looked at her hand, then back at Isabelle. "Thank you," she said in her hoarse voice. "It was a present. A long time ago." She put the pan on the stove but kept the wooden spoon.

Isabelle adjusted her robe beneath her and lifted a spoonful of oatmeal to her mouth. Miss Flora beamed while Miss Dora appraised her like a prison guard.

"Very good oatmeal," Isabelle said. "Aren't you going to have some?"

"We eat breakfast soon after rising," said Miss Flora. "We didn't hear you up and about then. If you don't have a good breakfast, you don't know what might go wrong during the day. Isn't that right, Dora?"

Miss Dora, spoon and pan now in hand, moved closer to Isabelle. "Yes, of course," she said.

Isabelle continued to eat. "Are you twins?" she asked.

"Goodness, no!" exclaimed Miss Flora. "Wouldn't that have been fun? We were born eleven months apart, weren't we, Dora?"

"We always have been."

"I was born on May Day, which is why Mother named me Flora. Dora arrived the next year on April Fools' Day."

"Very funny birthday," said Dora, her mouth a straight line.

When she was little, Isabelle had prayed for a baby sister or brother—she wasn't fussy—to appear. When her prayers weren't answered after what seemed like an eternity, she gave up.

She put her spoon in the empty bowl. "I should be going," she said, instead of the truth: I need to get away from here. "The oatmeal was great." The McCarthys were probably trying to be neighborly or kind, like the people who brought casseroles and doughnuts after Dad was gone. Besides, the sisters must have things to do, such as carrying bags of junk to the garage or making a pot roast for themselves or washing doilies.

Miss Dora plunked another spoonful of oatmeal in Isabelle's bowl.

Miss Flora looked at her sister, a question on her face. Miss Dora sent a message back with her eyebrows. "We hope that you'll accompany us on an outing very soon," said Miss Flora.

"An outing?" Isabelle replied.

"Do you enjoy outings, dear?"

"Of course she enjoys outings," Miss Dora answered before Isabelle could. "Who doesn't enjoy outings?"

"Let Little Girl speak," Miss Flora said as she smiled encouragement.

"What kind of outing?" Isabelle asked, wishing that she had held her hand over the bowl.

"I'm sure that it will be all right with your mother," said Miss Flora.

Weren't they going to tell her what it was? Isabelle spooned oatmeal into her mouth as fast as she could.

"We visit our brother, Fergus. Don't we, Dora?"

"On the twenty-third of every month—because he was born on the twenty-third. We're there, rain or shine."

"Where does he live?" Isabelle asked, a flicker of panic brushing her throat. The kitchen seemed warmer than it was when she started eating.

"He was our older brother, and he died before his time," said Miss Flora with a sigh. "Only eighty-four years old." As if suddenly remembering Isabelle's question, she added, "He's in the cemetery, dear."

Backing out of the kitchen, Isabelle bumped into a little table topped with a doily. "I have to finish unpacking now," she said. "Thank you for breakfast."

"You can use the fresh air," Miss Dora said. "It will do you good."

"Dora doesn't mean that we're going today," said Miss Flora. "We'll be going on Friday, won't we, Dora? You will love it, Little Girl. It's beautiful. The sweep of it and the birds and the statues. We usually bring a fresh flowerpot and pick up the last one. We like to change flowers, don't we, Dora? But the pots are getting too heavy for us to lift into the wagon."

Isabelle sneezed. "Excuse me," she said. "And I don't mean any disrespect, but my name is Isabelle, Miss Flora."

"Why, I know that! It's a lovely name! My, but you'll need some tea for that cold. I'll put the kettle on."

"I don't have a cold." Something scratched her throat. She tried to stifle the next sneeze, which escaped as a wet snort. "I have to go. I'll have tea upstairs," she said, knowing that she would rather drink pond scum than hot tea. "Thanks again for breakfast."

Isabelle took two steps at a time. What would Dad think of the McCarthys? He didn't hide from old people at weddings and family gatherings. He was as happy talking with Great-Aunt Cleo or Grandma's cousin Lloyd as anyone else. He was always happy, except for the days when he didn't get up in the morning. But Isabelle always put those days as far back in her mind as she could, even at the time they had happened.

After shutting the door upstairs, she locked it, knowing full well that no lock would keep the McCarthys away. She sneezed. Maybe she was allergic to doilies after all.

8
SAVED BY GRACE

In science class, Isabelle searched her pockets for a handkerchief or tissue that wasn't soaked. She failed, then sniffled as hard as she could and looked at the clock. In ten minutes she could dart into the girls' bathroom for some toilet paper. It was her only chance to load up before returning to Room 316, that is, as long as no nun saw her duck in there without permission. What did they think kids did in there, flushed textbooks down the toilet?

She leaned back in her desk seat and thought about Saturday afternoon. She and Margaret had walked to Lake Harriet, even though the day was damp and cold. Afterward they sat on stools at the soda fountain at McRay Pharmacy and wished they hadn't ordered cones, which made them colder. But it didn't matter. All that mattered was being with Margaret. Again this morning, she had picked her up for school. What a difference it made, walking together.

"Isabelle Day!" Sister Geraldine, the science teacher, startled Isabelle. "Continue, please."

Had someone been reading about a litmus test? Where had he left off? Wouldn't this be a good time for everyone to get up and start dropping those little pieces of paper in solution to determine the pH factor, as if anyone needed to know that? Isabelle glanced across the aisle at Phyllis Baker, who always followed each line with her finger.

Taking her cue from Phyllis, Isabelle stood and began to read. She must have hit the right spot; Sister Geraldine didn't correct her. Sister remained in the next aisle, looming over Ralph Longstreet, a criminal in training.

Isabelle's voice was the only sound except for the hissing of the radiator. If she hadn't been standing, she might have dropped off to sleep by now. Science class followed civics, which followed lunch and recess. It was a drowsy time. Some kids held their heads in their hands as if their necks had been snapped.

Isabelle paused at the end of a sentence in order to tip her head back and breathe in. As she gripped the science book with her right hand and continued to read, she again fished in her pocket. Her handkerchiefs were soggy enough to ring out.

Where was a box of tissues when you needed

one? In Milwaukee, a box was always perched on the teacher's desk. She read faster, hoping to quickly finish whatever Sister Geraldine determined to be an adequate portion of the chapter. Head tilted slightly back, Isabelle turned to sneak a glance at Sister. Sister Geraldine's eyes were riveted on her.

So Sister could see it, the liquid collecting at the end of one nostril, forming a bubble. Isabelle tried not to panic. What could she do? Wipe her nose on her bare arm? Isabelle paused for a huge, ineffective sniffle.

If one kid saw the snot bubble, life wouldn't be worth living. If one kid saw it, that kid's elbow would elbow another's ribs, fingers would jab backs, feet would kick legs under desks. Isabelle Day, snot bubbler. She might as well drown in it.

"Sister!" A scream erupted behind Isabelle. "Sister! A mouse just ran over my foot!"

As all heads turned to look at Grace, who sat in the middle of the row in the back of the room, Isabelle dropped into her seat. She crumpled a piece of notebook paper and wiped her nose with it.

Rosary beads ricocheting off each other under her scapular, Sister Geraldine raced to the cloakroom to arm herself with the broom. "Where, Grace?" she called. "Where did it go?"

"There!" Grace shouted. "Fourth row!"

Phyllis Baker screamed and beat a path to the

back door. Thomas Hardy—a star basketball player— leaped to the top of his desk while kids scampered past on the heels of Phyllis. Mary Ann McGraw hoisted herself to the top of the bookshelves beneath the windows. Charles Hager cackled as he pulled a pack of Camels out of his uniform shirt pocket and waved it at Sister's back.

Two rows away, Margaret didn't look perturbed. Isabelle waved at her with the notebook paper, then stuffed it in her pocket with the soggy hankies. She couldn't care about a mouse after blowing a snot bubble as big as her face.

Sister beat the broom on the floor beneath desks. "Do you see it, Grace?" she asked.

With one hand in front of her mouth and eyes open wide, Grace pointed to the front of the room. "There it is," she cried. "The tail, under your desk."

Sister flew up the aisle.

Isabelle wiped her nose on another piece of note- book paper and walked toward the back door. The room was now empty except for Sister and Grace.

"I saw it," Grace whispered as Isabelle approached.

"I know you saw it."

"No, I saw your trouble."

"What?"

"The trouble. The snot. I could see through it."

"You saw it?" Isabelle tried to process what Grace wasn't saying. "You mean there isn't a mouse?"

"No talking in the back of the room unless you know where the mouse is," Sister called.

Grace shook her head as she stroked imaginary whiskers on both sides of her face.

"No mouse?" mouthed Isabelle. "You made it up?"

Grace nodded.

"Thank you," Isabelle whispered. As she passed the long cloakroom on the way to the door, the bell rang. It hadn't saved her. Margaret's friend, Grace, had saved her. She hadn't thought that Grace liked her.

Isabelle plodded back to Sister Mary Mercy's room for religion. En route, she ducked into the bathroom for a wad of toilet paper. She didn't want to go to class. She wanted to go to Milwaukee. She wanted to go to Carol's house after school, and she wanted to sit at the dinner table with Mom and Dad after that. She did not want to live over the McCarthys and their doilies. She did not want to go to a cemetery for a visit.

But Grace had saved her from total humiliation. Imagine risking retaliation from Sister Geraldine for someone you didn't know.

Sister Geraldine scurried past on her way to Sister Mary Mercy's room, most likely to report the impertinence of such a mouse.

Isabelle could see the mouse in her mind's eye. It rose on its haunches, then clasped its little belly, its head dropping to its chest with laughter. Isabelle laughed silently with it. It reminded her of watching cartoons with Dad, except that she had made this one up. Dad would have loved to know about it. But he wouldn't. He was gone, as gone as a mouse that was never real.

9
BITTER RAIN

Isabelle and Margaret walked with Grace until they came to her street.

"I never saw it," Margaret said. "I was trying to count Ed Svoboda's neck hairs to stay awake."

"It was a doozy," said Grace, "and transparent. It was like looking through wavy glass."

"Gross," said Margaret. "I can't believe that Sister didn't call on someone else."

"She was in a trance," Isabelle said, laughing, although there hadn't been anything funny about it. How did this happen? she wondered. My snot almost makes the five o'clock news, and I'm kind of happy about it now.

"See you tomorrow," Margaret said to Grace as she turned the corner.

"See you," Isabelle echoed. Grace wasn't the kind of person you could hug. A little impetuous and a little impertinent, Grace wore a mild repellent. Whether she wanted to maintain privacy or protect herself, Isabelle couldn't guess.

Is Grace your best friend? Isabelle wanted to ask Margaret. She must be. But Isabelle didn't want to hear the answer. She needed Margaret. She didn't want to think about alliances.

After she said good-bye to Margaret, Isabelle crossed the street and walked through the front porch and into the small hallway. She stood for a moment, surveying the space where she had handed out candy. Halloween—so recent—seemed distant. So quickly, she had a friend across the street and, maybe, another who had saved her. For a second, Isabelle felt a foreign sensation. Could she be happy? Is that what made her feel lighter?

Out of nowhere, reality shook her as forcibly as if two hands clutched her shoulders. You had friends. You had a house with Dad in it. Enormous losses, paltry gains.

The resentment and sorrow of Halloween crept back. This is what Dad did to me, she thought. I am two people: one who has lost everything and one who pretends that new friends can make up for it.

Isabelle's nose dripped. She wiped it on her jacket sleeve, then lifted her other arm and smeared the tears that were dropping.

"Little Girl!" Miss Flora stood at her door.

"Her name is Isabelle," said Miss Dora from the living room. "You know her name."

"Little Isabelle! Of course! Please come in for some cocoa. We could all use a spot of cocoa on such a dreary day."

"I have to go on an errand, so I can't come in now." Isabelle put her books on the first step that led upstairs. "I'll see you another time."

For once, Miss Flora didn't cast a net of cajoling words over her. Isabelle turned and walked outside, where the air felt colder than it had moments earlier. She walked to the end of the block and turned right, away from the route that led to school.

Lakewood Cemetery, caught only in glimpses earlier, loomed one block away. Its monuments and markers clung to the swells and dips.

When she was little, she and Dad had driven past a cemetery on a bright winter day. The snow sparkled in the sunshine. "I know what that is," she told him. "It's where dead people go."

"Only their bodies," Dad answered. "The soul lives on."

"Just the heads go to heaven?" Isabelle said.

When she was older, she and Dad and Mom laughed about the question. Now it didn't seem funny.

Isabelle buttoned her jacket up to her chin. Again she imagined telling Dad about the snot. The story would become legendary, a touchstone in which she, Isabelle, triumphed, and Grace took her rightful place as a humorous yet minor character.

Now the story was erased as cold rain fell gingerly, and Isabelle's pleasure in Margaret and Grace felt desperate. On the ground, leaves not yet weighted with moisture performed a defiant dance, rising and circling on gusts of wind. Cars driving past the cemetery seemed to accelerate as if to deny that such a place existed.

Isabelle walked on the sidewalk next to the iron fence. She hadn't saved Dad. Mom hadn't either. Who was there to blame?

10

CEMETERY DELEGATION

"**D**o you think you can do it?" Mom asked Isabelle the evening before the cemetery visit with the McCarthys. "You know you don't have to."

Do what? Could she say that to Mom? *Go to a cemetery?* Weren't they busy pretending they had never been in one? Wasn't Mom supposed to protect her?

"Flora and Dora are so excited that you're going to help them with the flowerpot," Mom continued.

"It's settled, then." Isabelle brimmed with self-pity.

"It's so close. It shouldn't take long." Mom spoke rapidly, almost with desperation. "And you're going to Margaret's today. You love going to Margaret's. You'll have such a good time."

After school, Isabelle ran up the stairs without worrying about noise. The McCarthys already expected her. She changed out of her uniform, poured cereal into a bowl, and ate standing up as she stared at Margaret's house. Should she put on extra socks? No, just hurry downstairs and get this over with. The cold, damp air had sliced through her on the way home, but the McCarthys wouldn't dawdle at graveside today. The sun—hidden behind a foreboding gray wall since morning—would set soon, taking its weak light with it.

Miss Flora opened the door immediately after Isabelle rapped. "We don't want to make you wait, Little Isabelle. We're as ready as can be, aren't we, Dora?"

"I think that's apparent."

Each sister wore a dark cloth coat and a small hat fit so snugly that the hatpins lacked purpose, and each had a scarf tucked securely in the neck of her coat. Their hands were mittened and their feet were shod in zip-up rubber boots. Miss Flora held a small black purse.

"The wagon is in the backyard," she said. She pointed to the squat pot of marigolds that bloomed in the dining room. Isabelle walked to it and lifted. How could they have handled this by themselves?

"This might be the last time for flowers this year," Miss Dora said. "But marigolds don't mind a little bracing weather."

Bracing weather? The flowers would be battered before they reached the cemetery entrance. Isabelle dutifully lugged the pot out the door that Miss Flora held open. "We'll leave this sturdy pot there and start seeds in the spring," Miss Flora whispered, as if they were involved in espionage.

Isabelle pulled the wagon between the sisters, only one hand clad in a mitten, the other having disappeared somewhere between the upstairs and downstairs. As the procession approached the cemetery, Miss Flora said in a solemn voice, "There he is. On the rise."

Their brother was one of a multitude of markers that looked like stamps on the swell. Around him, the wind whipped the bare trees whose trunks held to the ground resolutely.

The cemetery gates were open, flung wide.

"We climb, right?" said Isabelle.

The wind threatened to blow them off course. Isabelle parked the wagon at the gate and stuck her arms out, making chicken wings. "Hold on," she said. "Link together."

Straining against the wind, they reached the gravesite. One hand in her pocket, Isabelle ran back for the wagon. She then placed the pot in front of the marker that read, "Fergus Michael McCarthy, 1874–1958."

"That's a very nice marker," Isabelle said because no one else spoke. A smaller container lay tipped next to the gravestone, the choked flowers impossible to identify.

"Thank you, Little Isabelle," said Miss Flora. "Fergus would have enjoyed knowing you and your mother."

Miss Dora led them in prayer, and then Miss Flora said, "Fergus, we are so fortunate to have the dearest girl living upstairs. Her name is Little Isabelle." She giggled, "I mean Isabelle, and she's come with us today. Would you like to say hello, Isabelle?"

All she had offered to do was haul soon-to-die flowers. Now she was supposed to have a conversation with the McCarthys' dead brother?

Miss Flora dabbed at her eyes with a lacy handkerchief.

Isabelle stared at the marker, then looked upward. When she was younger, she had imagined heaven to be on the other side of the blue sky. Sometimes she would lie on her back, waiting to see someone—Grandma Olive or maybe a saint—accidentally slip into view. Grandma or the saint would be as surprised as she was. There would be a wave and a quick exit. Today she had no intention of seeing Fergus McCarthy, but she might as well address his tombstone.

"Your sisters are very nice, Mr. McCarthy, and I'm sure you were, too. Amen."

"Fergus was buried in his best wool suit," Miss Flora said, now smiling at the marker.

"Not like that penny-pinching Mr. Unkowski who had his family buy a new suit for his wake and then return it to the department store," said Miss Dora.

"I thought they couldn't return it because of the embalming fluid that leaked," Miss Flora said.

"Either way, he was a crook."

"Are we ready to go?" asked Isabelle, as she switched her mitten to the colder hand.

"We must say a prayer for your dear father, too," said Miss Flora.

Isabelle preferred not to say a prayer for her dear father at this time and place. Instead of saying so, she stuffed her hands as far as they would go in her pockets.

The sisters clasped their hands and lowered their eyelids. After silent prayers were finished, Miss Flora said, "Let's take the old flowers home now."

The cemetery gates looked different this time. They were closed. Isabelle tried to open them, first one side, then the other.

Although she could move each side a few inches, even a person as small as Miss Flora couldn't escape through the opening.

"I think we're locked in," she said.

"You don't say!" said Miss Flora.

"The cemetery closes at four o'clock in the winter," Miss Dora said, as if that should be apparent to anyone.

"But we didn't get here until after four o'clock," said Isabelle. Since when did winter officially start in November?

"Yes, Dora, that's what the sign reads," Miss Flora said. "But Jimmy is almost always late. He's hardly ever at this entrance by closing time." She looked at Isabelle. "Last winter we were locked in until a man who lives nearby called the police. Wasn't I glad to be wearing my wool stockings that time!"

"Why did we come so late if you knew it might be closed?" asked Isabelle. Her heart thumped under her jacket as if trying to escape.

"We usually come earlier in the day, but we wanted to wait for you," Miss Flora said.

"You'll have to go for help now," said her sister.

"Help?"

"Climb out and bring back help," said Miss Dora, as if help were a person with a ring of keys who lived across the street.

"How?" Isabelle pictured herself on the couch, drinking cocoa with the afghan tucked under her toes.

Miss Dora motioned toward the fence with her head. "You look like a climber to me." She looked uncertain, almost worried behind her mask of a face.

"I'm sure that you can do it, dear," said Miss Flora. "Once when we were locked in, a young man scaled the fence and waited with us. He alerted the police first, of course. Wasn't he a nice young man, Dora?"

"Yes, he was," Dora said. She turned to Isabelle. "Now you'd best begin."

Isabelle considered the smooth vertical bars, washed by the rain that had begun to spit on them. One horizontal bar ran through the middle of the side-by-side gates. Isabelle stretched her left leg upward. With some difficulty, she maneuvered her foot onto the horizontal bar.

"We'll push the rest of you up," said Miss Flora encouragingly.

As Isabelle tried to pull herself up, each sister pushed one side of Isabelle's rear end. The only way to get the tiny, ineffectual fingers off her was to scale the gate. Isabelle lifted herself up so that her other foot rested on the bar, too.

"She's a little Houdini, Little Isabelle is," said Miss Flora, her mittened hands clapping a muffled applause.

From her perch, Isabelle turned sideways to avoid the spikes, a decorative defense. She dropped to the other side, falling so hard that her heels hurt as if whacked.

"Now what? Go home and call for help?" Her hands ached with cold.

The sisters looked at each other as if questioning Isabelle's intelligence.

"Go," said Miss Dora, "to the other side." She pointed at what looked like a prison wall. "Park police."

"Hurry, dear, hurry," Miss Flora implored. As she

spoke, she removed her mittens, put them in her pocket, and took a compact—a small, round disk—from her purse and proceeded to powder her nose. She looked in the little mirror again before closing the compact.

Isabelle watched, incredulous. It was time to escape.

11

RESCUE MISSION

Across the street, Isabelle ran along a wall until she came to the sprawling building and found the entrance. Inside, in front of her, an elevator with bars stood untended. With two corridors from which to choose, Isabelle turned right and paused at the first door. A man in a police uniform sat behind an enormous desk.

"Excuse me," Isabelle said. "I'm looking for help."

"You're in the right place. This is the park police building." The man had a blond crew cut and ruddy complexion. He looked strong enough to lift his desk.

"My neighbors sent me here. You see, they're locked in the cemetery."

"Are they alive?"

"They were a few minutes ago." Sometimes it was hard to tell when adults were trying to be funny.

"Are you sure about that?"

"They're not permanent residents of the cemetery, if that's what you mean." She looked at the nameplate on the desk: Officer Daniel Ryan.

"How did they get in if the gates are locked?" He rummaged through his top drawer and withdrew a ring of keys.

"We just walked in. The gates were open a little while ago."

"It sounds as if you were set up," Officer Ryan said, smiling broadly. "Are you sure that we should let them out? Or should we teach those McCarthy sisters a lesson?"

"Do you know them?" Did a park police officer know everyone in the city?

"This isn't the first time they've been locked in."

"Maybe the next time you could give them a ticket or something."

"All the citations in the book won't stop them from being the McCarthy sisters," said Officer Ryan. "They're not the only ones who've been locked in."

"But they're regulars?"

"You could say that. Maybe two or three times a year." He stood and pulled a puffy police jacket from a coatrack behind his desk. "I'll pick the sisters up and give them a ride home. Actually I enjoy catching up with them. Do you want a ride?"

"I only live a block from here," Isabelle said. "I'll walk. They have a wagon, too."

"I'll flip it in the trunk, maybe drive them around

the lake. They don't get out as much as they used to when I started here." He called loudly to someone that Isabelle couldn't see. "Chuck, I'm off to rescue the McCarthys. See you bright and early."

"Thanks," Isabelle said as she started for the door.

"Thanks for sounding the alarm," he said. "Just watch the clock if you make the trip with them again."

Warmed by running and her time in the police station, Isabelle sat for a few minutes on a swing sheltered by trees in the empty Lyndale Farmstead Park. What a name. It wasn't on Lyndale Avenue and there wasn't a farm.

Tonight she would write to Carol and make the incident in the cemetery sound funny. But it wasn't.

Upstairs in the duplex, the door stood ajar. "I'm having a cup of tea," Mom called from the kitchen when Isabelle entered the living room and kicked off her boots. "You were gone a long time. Would you like cocoa? I'm just going to start supper."

By the time Isabelle had hung up her coat and put her mitten on the radiator, Mom was stirring milk into the mixture of cocoa and sugar.

"What happened to your hands?" said Mom.

"That's the least of my troubles."

"It was that bad?"

"Yes."

"I saw your mitten on the steps when I came in. But I thought you'd be right back. Of course, I didn't know when you'd left."

"We had a problem."

"You couldn't get in?"

"We couldn't get out."

"You were locked in the cemetery? Please tell me you're kidding."

"I'm not. I had to crawl over a gate made of icicles. Then I had to find a policeman who had a key."

"The park police building," Mom said, a dreamy look on her face. "Every fall there was a mum show in the attached greenhouses. Mums, all colors, all sorts. I can still smell them."

"Mom, I'm talking about the McCarthys. They basically kidnapped me. I almost froze to the cemetery gate."

A sharp knock sounded at the front door.

"That is definitely not a McCarthy knock," Isabelle said.

"Keep stirring," said Mom, handing Isabelle the wooden spoon. "I'll go see."

Isabelle recognized the deep voice. She strained to hear.

"You won't believe who's here," Mom called back to Isabelle.

Isabelle turned off the burner and walked into the living room. Officer Ryan, the police officer who had allegedly freed the McCarthys by this time, stood just outside the doorframe.

"It's Danny Ryan, my friend Cindy's little brother," Mom said.

"Hi," said Isabelle.

"I had no idea this was your mom," Officer Ryan said. He looked too tall to fit through the door. "Your friends downstairs asked me to make sure that you were home safely."

"I made it."

"Cindy and I are having lunch tomorrow. What a coincidence, seeing you," Mom said.

"She told me that you were moving back. In some ways, it's the same neighborhood. In others, it's not. You used to live on the other side of the church, right?"

"Yes."

Officer Ryan cleared his throat. "You've had a bad time of it, Mary Lou. I'm sorry for that."

"I know you are. Thanks for stopping by to check on Isabelle."

After Officer Ryan bounded down the stairs and Isabelle and Mom went back to the kitchen, Mom turned on the burner under the teakettle. "Do you want me to warm the cocoa?" she asked.

"No, it's okay."

"All I have to do is turn the burner on for a minute."

"I said that I am okay," Isabelle said, her voice rising with each syllable.

Mom looked back at the stove and continued talking as if someone had asked her a question.

"Really, Isabelle, Danny was the scrawniest little boy I ever saw. Perpetually damp, too, as if he had a cold from birth. It's impossible to separate him from that boy, even though he's such a nice-looking man."

How could any man look good after Dad? How could Mom even notice?

Thinking about the cemetery was almost better than thinking about Officer Ryan, even as a slimy child. She should have asked Margaret to come to the cemetery. If Margaret had been there, they could have made it sound funny after the fact. Isabelle didn't think she had the drive to do it on her own. All she wanted to do was forget this day.

12
HOSPITAL BOUND

On the following Friday, Miss Flora sat at the dining room table upstairs and cried softly into her handkerchief, a few tears barely missing the tuna casserole on her plate.

"It's just that we've never been apart for long," she said. "And I'm so worried about her."

When Isabelle had arrived home from school two days earlier, the lower duplex was silent—no Miss Flora chattering, no pans rattling, no needle scratching a phonograph record. That evening, Miss Flora's daughter called to tell Mom that Miss Dora had slipped in the backyard and broken her hip. Until then, Isabelle hadn't realized that one McCarthy might be more trouble than two.

"You see her in the hospital, don't you?" Isabelle said.

"Oh, yes, dear. But only during visiting hours."

She blew her noise delicately. "Dora is on pain medicine and barely recognized me today. I'll go tomorrow."

"It's so hard on both of you," said Mom. "You need all your strength. Dora will depend on you when she's alert."

She turned to Isabelle. "You're going to Margaret's, aren't you?"

"Now don't stay here on my account," Miss Flora said. Stray hairs had wriggled out of her bun, and her nose looked shiny under the overhead light. "You run along to Margaret's."

She must know that I don't want to stay and watch her cry, Isabelle thought. Of course, that hadn't stopped her from kidnapping me for the cemetery disaster.

"Mrs. Day," said Miss Flora between sniffles, "I hope that you won't think me greedy, but one bite of this chocolate cake might cheer Dora up—if she's alert tomorrow. May I wrap a small piece?"

"I'm going now," Isabelle said, pushing away from the table. Miss Flora could be such an optimist, imagining that a piece of cake could make Miss Dora whole and happy.

Mom walked into the kitchen and returned. "I hate to think of you busing to the hospital in this weather," she said as she ripped off a sheet of wax paper. "I'd drive you if I had a car."

"I've taken the streetcar—I mean the bus, now—in

all kinds of weather since I was a little girl. I like getting around on my own as much as I can. But my own Margaret is going to pick me up tomorrow. I only hope that Dora will be home soon."

Dad's mom had died of pneumonia in the hospital after breaking her hip. Grandma Olive had never gotten out of bed, much less walked, after she fell.

"Say hi to Miss Dora from me," Isabelle said. She walked to Mom and gave her a hasty peck on the cheek that she offered.

Miss Flora would probably be upstairs regularly. Yesterday Mrs. Underwood across the street had sent a Dutch oven of beef stew for dinner. Miss Flora had insisted on sharing it with Mom and Isabelle. Food arrived from other neighbors today, the tuna casserole and a chicken potpie. Miss Flora, who said that she couldn't eat it all if she lived for a hundred years, asked Isabelle to carry the food upstairs.

The phone rang, and Isabelle answered. "Hurry up," said Margaret. "Grace is already here."

Minutes later, Isabelle stepped into Margaret's living room. "We didn't get to this on the way home," Grace said, stepping in front of Margaret. "In geography, we're supposed to remember what we learned about Africa in third grade—and we don't remember any of it—and today you stood at the pull-down map and showed us Uganda."

"My dad and I used to look at the atlas together,"

Isabelle said, instantly wishing that she hadn't brought him up.

Margaret's mother walked into the room. "Hello, Isabelle," she said, wearing her slow, sweet smile. "How are you? How is Dora?"

"I'm fine. Miss Dora isn't very conscious, I guess."

"What about me?" said Grace. "You didn't ask me how I was."

"I forget that you don't live here," answered Margaret's father, reading the afternoon newspaper in a far corner of the living room. He smiled at Isabelle with such unaffected good humor that she couldn't speak. She blinked away the picture of Dad grinning.

"Miss Flora is really upset without her sister," Isabelle said to Margaret's mother.

One twin rode into the living room in a child-size jeep, her knees going up and down as she pedaled. The other twin walked next to her, balancing a tinfoil crown on a pillow.

"For the princess," said the twin with the crown. She stared at the floor rather than Isabelle, as if awestruck in the presence of royalty.

"You can have a ride," said the driver twin. "You can sit on the back."

The back of the jeep looked as if it could accommodate a small stuffed animal.

"Thank you," Isabelle said. "But I'm a little too big. I'll wear the crown." She knelt in front of the shyer twin, who used both hands to place it on Isabelle's head. Isabelle stood slowly in order to balance her crown.

"The jeep was Mark's," Margaret said. "They call it a carriage."

"I call it 'time to leave,'" said Grace.

"Thank you very much," Isabelle said to the twins. She curtsied solemnly, holding her head erect.

In the basement, seated in front of a small television balanced on a peach crate, Isabelle asked Margaret, "How can you tell them apart?"

"It's easy when you've lived with them their whole lives."

"Think of them as the United States and Canada," said Grace. "I went to Winnipeg once. At first, it seems the same as Minneapolis. But after you've been there a while, it feels different."

"I've never been to Winnipeg," Isabelle said.

A scream from upstairs broke through. For a moment, the girls stared at each other. Then Grace jumped up and took the steps two at a time, Margaret on Grace's heels. Isabelle followed, startled and, at the same time, annoyed at leaving the sagging couch with cushions that had molded to her body.

In the living room, one twin sat in the jeep, staring at the screaming twin whose hand was being wrapped in a dish towel by their mother, who was on her knees. Their father slipped into his jacket as he emerged from the front hall closet.

"Looks as if she'll need stitches," he said.

"What happened?" Margaret asked.

"My hand got stuck," said Karen, the driver twin, pointing to something near the wheel well. "Kathleen pulled it out. Then her fingers got stuck in there. Poor little baby."

Blood began to blossom on the dish towel around Kathleen's hand.

"You'd think they have enough to do without amputating each other's limbs," Grace whispered to Isabelle.

"Mom's going to hold down the fort," said Margaret's dad.

"Her mom doesn't drive," Grace interpreted for Isabelle.

Margaret's dad pocketed his keys. "If you girls want to ride along, you can help calm the patient."

"Oh, Hal," said Margaret's mother. "I should go."

"Someone should be here when Mark gets home," he said. "Do you girls want to come or stay here?"

"We could stay here and watch Karen," said Isabelle. She wanted to be in the basement waiting for *The Twilight Zone* to come on.

Kathleen clung to her mother's neck, trying to suck the index finger of her good hand as she sobbed. Her curled posture—one arm flung about her mother and her body nestled close—looked like that of a baby monkey.

"My life is spent watching babies," said Grace. "Let's go."

Margaret's dad leaned down, and Kathleen—limp as a rag doll—allowed herself to be transferred from mother to father.

13
BREAKING THE RULES

By the time they reached the emergency room—where the lights were bright enough to resurrect faded scars—the girls had completed several rounds of "Old McDonald" for Kathleen's benefit. A gibbon, opossum, and wombat found their way into the song. Kathleen remained silent except for an occasional sniffle.

"She's probably in shock without her other half," Grace said.

Holding Kathleen in the crook of his arm, her father followed a nurse through a door. "If you wander, check back here every twenty minutes or so," he said to the girls. The door swung shut.

"This looks like a prison hospital," Isabelle said quietly, looking away as a man whose facial cuts were bleeding through a towel was wheeled past them.

"I'm getting bored," said Grace.

"I know what we can do," Isabelle said. "We can visit Miss Dora. She's here."

Margaret and Grace stared at her. "Brilliant," said Grace. "I can't think of anything more fun except for watching grass grow."

"It's something," Isabelle said. She stood, quickly ran out of the room and down a hall, read a sign, and hurried back. "We still have a little more than half an hour. We just have to figure out where she is."

"Why do we want to see her?" Grace asked Margaret. "I never wanted to see her when she was across the street from you."

"What else do we have to do?" said Isabelle. "Besides, it will give me something to talk to Miss Flora about besides oatmeal."

"Guts," Grace said to Margaret. "Your friend has guts."

Isabelle marched ahead. "This way," she said. They approached the information desk in a lobby of marble walls and columns that held the ceiling up. A bent, elderly man stepped from the elevator, leaning on his cane as he took small, careful steps, his polka-dot bow tie almost parallel to the ground.

At his son's funeral, Grandpa Day had gripped a cane with white knuckles. Isabelle pushed the image away.

The nurse at the information desk was crowned with a small starched cap secured by bobby pins.

"I'm Dora McCarthy's granddaughter," Isabelle began. "Could you please give me my grandmother's room number?"

The nurse slid her glance from Isabelle to Margaret and Grace. Leaning toward them, she asked, "And which one of you drove here?"

"My father did," Isabelle said, straightening her spine indignantly. "He's in the emergency room with my little sister who cut her finger and needs stitches. My father's name is Hal Morris. He said that we should try to see our grandmother before visiting hours are over because he probably won't be able to see her tonight."

Isabelle looked from the nurse to the black telephone, a sentry on the desk. "My little sister's name is Kathleen Morris."

The nurse placed her hand on the phone, then changed course and ran her finger down a patient list on the desk. "Main Two West," she said. "You may ask the station nurse about your grandmother, but visiting hours are just about over."

"Maybe the station nurse will understand how important it is for our grandmother to know we're here," Grace said with a toss of her ponytail.

The nurse looked as if she would rather give a shot to each of the girls than listen further. "I can change my mind about letting you talk to the station nurse," she said.

"Thank you for your help," Isabelle said, trying to make her smile look sincere.

In the elevator, the girls laughed until they reached the second floor, after which they bit the insides of their cheeks and tried to avoid looking at each other.

"I can't remember why we want to see her," Margaret whispered in the hallway.

"Seeing her," said Grace, "is not the point. Getting in is the point."

"Shhh," Isabelle shushed.

Arms crossed, a nurse stood in the hallway with her back to them. The man and woman with whom she spoke didn't pay attention to the girls, who moved toward the Main Two West sign. Isabelle, Margaret, and Grace slipped into the ward and stood against a wall.

Metal beds on casters were spread out in a U formation, some of the beds flanked by drawn curtains. A touch of streetlight seeped in around the window shades, highlighting limbs suspended from hardware above the bed frames.

"There must be twenty broken bodies in here," whispered Grace.

Isabelle stared, shot through with the idiocy of her plan. Why were they here? The nurse's desk sat empty. If only the nurse had been at her station or in the ward, this ludicrous idea might have been stopped by now.

"Is that a leg up there?" Grace said.

"Quiet," Margaret whispered. "How can we tell which one is Miss Dora?"

A voice rose from one of the beds. "Who's there? Is that you, Morty?" The bed rustled slightly.

"Morty isn't here," Grace whispered loudly in the direction of the voice. "Please don't wake the other patients, or we'll have to put you in the hall."

With her eyes growing accustomed to the near darkness, Isabelle raised her eyebrows at Margaret as if to say, "Grace has nerve." Margaret rolled her eyes as if to say, "She's going too far."

"We should drop," Grace said. "Some of them might see us."

The girls crouched. A crank at the bottom of the nearest bed became visible as their eyes adjusted to the dark.

"I think I can find her now," said Isabelle. She crawled to the end of the first bed on the right, pulled herself to her knees, and stared at a sleeping woman who was not Miss Dora. The woman's chins moved up and down as she snored gently.

"Not this one," she whispered. She scooted to the next bed, pausing to look back at the hallway.

"They must give them sleeping pills with dinner," she heard Grace whisper to Margaret.

Isabelle faced the next head on a pillow. The woman's skin glowed waxen, and her straight nose rose from her face like the highest point on a death mask. Isabelle shuddered, then crawled back to Margaret and Grace. "This might take a few minutes," she said. Traveling by floor made her long for a bath.

To entertain Grace and Margaret, Isabelle dropped to her stomach and, swinging her legs behind her, snake-style, pulled herself along on her elbows. The stifled laughter from Margaret and Grace fueled her.

"I know that you're here, Morty," cried the woman again. "I've been waiting for you."

"What did I tell you?" Grace replied in a loud whisper in the woman's direction. "One more peep and you're out in the hall."

Isabelle wriggled to the next bed and the next, squinting at each face. Each woman slept on her back, hands on her stomach or chest, prepared for a coffin lid to lower. Isabelle tried to banish the image by picturing a sunny day, but she couldn't summon it. She pulled herself up at the next bed. She could at least find Miss Dora and report back. That is, if the pounding of her heart didn't wake everyone in Main Two West.

The thin line of streetlight at the bottom of a shade struck the hands on top of a blanket. The gold band on Miss Dora's ring finger, adorned by the speck of amethyst, winked at Isabelle. But instead of Miss Dora, a tent rose above the site where her face and chest should be. It climbed about three feet from the bedclothes, and a zipper offered access to Miss Dora's upper half.

"Miss Dora," Isabelle whispered. Horrified, she couldn't think of anything to say, not that Miss Dora could hear her. "Miss Dora, this is Isabelle, your neighbor. Get well, please."

Isabelle lowered herself. As she did, she imagined that Miss Dora's left hand rose slightly and fell back to the blanket. Isabelle couldn't be sure. But just in case the hand had been trying to send a message, Isabelle said softly, "Yes, you'll be home soon." Then she crawled toward the ward entrance. In the distance, metal wheels squeaked in time to a gentle sloshing. When the sound of the wheels stopped, a wet mop slapped the marble floor in the hallway.

"Morty, is that you?" the voice called. "Morty?"

A hand tugged Isabelle. "Let's go," said Margaret. "We have to get out of here before the nurse shows up."

In the hallway, the elevator chimed. Almost blinded by the light, Isabelle followed Grace and Margaret as they rushed toward the exit sign.

14
NO TURNING BACK

At the bottom of the first floor stairwell, Grace asked Isabelle, "What was that thing back there?"

"Some kind of tent." Isabelle wondered if she would ever catch her breath. "I couldn't see much of her that wasn't covered."

"How did you know it was her?"

"Her ring." The tiny amethyst had looked odd on the gnarled hand.

"I smell something funny," Margaret said. "Like that ward."

"It's me," said Isabelle, as they all sampled the air. "The disinfectant or something almost made me gag. It's on my hands and my clothes."

"We probably all smell like it," Margaret said.

In the emergency room waiting area, the girls sat silently until Margaret's dad and Kathleen appeared.

"Did they fix you?" Grace asked.

"Sewed me up." Kathleen held her bandaged finger for everyone to admire. Dry tear tracks contrasted with her smile. Approval received, she put her arms around her father's neck.

"Did you get tired of waiting?" Margaret's dad asked.

"We went to see Miss Dora," said Margaret.

"You got in? Isn't it too late?"

"Nobody stopped us. But we didn't exactly see her. She was in some kind of a tent."

"Not even a hair," Grace said. "Someone is probably doing experiments on the upper half of her body in a laboratory in the basement."

"Do you write for *The Twilight Zone*?" Margaret asked.

"Maybe."

"If she's in a tent, she probably has pneumonia or, at the very least, is having trouble breathing." Margaret's dad shifted Kathleen to his other arm. "Her sister must know." He looked at his little daughter. "Should we take these girls home? It's past their bedtime."

"Good," Kathleen said, watching the girls from her perch. The word "bedtime" prompted an involuntary response; she put her index finger in her mouth. "Yuck," she said, eyeing the bandaged finger suspiciously.

After Grace was dropped off, Margaret's dad put

his car to bed in the garage and carried Kathleen into the house through the back door. Margaret walked Isabelle to the front yard and faced the duplex. No light shone downstairs. Upstairs, lights blazed.

"I think it's colder than when we left," Isabelle said, hugging herself.

The street looked as if it were closed for the night, with everyone buttoned up in the houses and not even a cat in sight.

"Did your mom leave all those lights on for you?" Margaret asked.

"Yes, plus she's getting ready for my grandparents. They're coming from Hovland, up north, for the weekend." Mom wouldn't even know that she had left Margaret's and gone to the hospital.

"Is that why you moved here? To be closer to your grandparents?"

"That's some of it. My mom grew up here. But her parents moved after my mom got married."

"So why didn't she move to her parents' town instead of Minneapolis?"

"She wanted to be in a city where she could get a job right away, someplace bigger."

"Someplace that isn't Milwaukee?"

Isabelle looked at Margaret, now slightly blurred by snowflakes that came between them. "My dad died in Milwaukee."

"I know."

"If your dad died, you probably wouldn't want to stay in your house either."

"Probably not. I don't know."

"I'm glad we moved." She wasn't glad. She had never wanted to leave the brick house. But every grown-up who talked to her made her want to cry. She wanted to punch every kid who stared at her.

Isabelle's toes began to complain about the cold. Even though it was late, she wished that Margaret would ask her to come to her house.

"It must be really hard being in a new place with just your mom." Margaret paused. "Did you know your dad was going to die?"

Isabelle shook her head no. She waved good-bye. Then she moved her fingers up and down in a second wave, trying to be friendly without words, without her voice cracking.

At home, Mom stood in the kitchen, frosting an angel food cake. "Did you have a good time at Margaret's?" she asked. She looked expectant, hoping for a cheerful report.

"Miss Dora has pneumonia, I think."

Mom held the knife with pink icing in the air. "How do you know?"

"Margaret's sister sliced her finger, so we went to the hospital with her and her dad. It was the hospital that Miss Dora was in, so I thought I would go see her. She was in something that might be an oxygen tent."

"Poor Dora," said Mom, lowering herself to a chair. The raised knife in her hand brushed her hair, frosting a small section of it. "Poor Flora."

Poor us, Isabelle said to herself, leaving Mom and the partially frosted cake in the kitchen, the ritual of the good-night kiss forgotten.

15

HISTORY OF LOSS

The next Sunday, the sun shone brightly. Miss Flora left to see her sister following one o'clock dinner in the upper duplex. Miss Dora was "out of the woods," she said. Mom washed the dishes and Isabelle dried. Isabelle set the dinner plates and dessert plates noisily on top of each other so as to disguise the emptiness.

"Are you going to see Margaret this afternoon?" Mom asked as she tipped the basin, allowing the dishwater to race to the drain.

"Maybe. Unless her relatives are here. We didn't make any plans."

"Sundays are a little quiet."

Sundays weren't quiet with Dad. After church, Mom removed her sparkly screw-on earrings that left tiny indentations in her lobes. In the summer, sometimes they went to the beach or on a picnic, bringing Carol. In winter they skated or built snow forts. Mom cooked a chicken or lasagna or chow mein that they ate in the dining room with the bay window.

"I think I'll go for a walk," Isabelle said.

"Do you want me to come?"

"Now that I think about it, maybe I won't go."

"Are you having a hard day?"

"No." Every day was a hard day.

Mom let out a long, uneven sigh. She pulled out a kitchen chair and dropped into it, placing her elbows on her knees as if she were her own prop. She stared, although she didn't appear to be looking at anything. "I've been waiting for a magic wand to appear," she said in a flat voice. "To make things the way they were. But I'm giving up on that." The wind picked up and shook the windows a little.

"I changed my mind. I'm going to see if Margaret can come out," Isabelle said. She walked through the dining room to get her jacket, to get away.

"I wish I could be like Miss Flora," said Mom, her voice dull. "She says that she understands loss."

Isabelle zipped up her jacket and took a scarf and mittens from the closet, then stood in the middle of the living room. The sun that streamed through the window didn't fool her. Even the blue sky looked chilled. She walked slowly back to the kitchen, aware that her feet had other ideas. But it might feel worse to leave Mom like this than to escape. She knew that guilt would cover her like glue.

"Why does she understand?"

"She told me about her life because I asked her."

Isabelle unzipped her jacket.

"She married a man named Charles who worked for the railroad," Mom said, staring straight ahead. "They had a baby girl, Mary Catherine. In the meantime, Dora married her sweetheart, Laurence, but he died soon after."

"This is cheerful."

"Flora and her husband asked Dora to live with them. Soon there were three more girls: Helen, Alice, and Dora, the baby. Miss Dora adored the girls."

"Are we almost to the happy ending?"

Mom stood up to stare out the window above the sink. "An 'unwelcome visitor' arrived, Flora said. Influenza. Imagine this, Isabelle."

At least Mom still knew her name. Maybe this was good for Mom, to wrap herself in someone else's misery.

"Late in the afternoon, every weekday, the girls lined up at the kitchen window, waiting for their father to appear in the backyard after getting off the streetcar."

Looking as if her legs couldn't hold her, Mom sat down again. "Little Dora was the first to get sick and die. So, at first, the line at the window didn't change very much. But then Helen and Alice died within three days of each other. Their father continued to look up at the window where Mary Catherine waited. But she died, too. After that, the girls' father hung his head when he came in the backyard."

"Wasn't there any medicine for it, the influenza?"

"No. This was the pandemic in 1918. Oddly, healthy adults were usually hit hardest—but not in Flora's family." Mom wiped her eyes. "Flora told me that Dora said, 'I refuse to let you die of a broken heart.'"

"Miss Dora said that? At least they had baby Margaret."

Mom nodded. "Yes, later."

"I'm going to see my Margaret now," Isabelle said. She didn't want to be in the same room with Miss Flora's story, even though it had happened a long time ago. She didn't want to hear about how no one had died of a broken heart. She still might.

"That's good." Mom stood and took her school folders from the counter. Isabelle was heartened, seeing Mom still responsive to the world of duty even though she looked like a zombie.

"Is her daughter, Margaret, nice to her?" Isabelle said.

"When we don't hear Flora and Dora on Sundays, they're with Margaret's family. Today was an exception. And Margaret calls her mother every weekday after *The Guiding Light* because she knows she'll be waiting as soon as she turns the TV off."

"Why do Miss Flora and Miss Dora visit their brother's grave but not the little girls'?"

"I don't know. Maybe they do and we don't know it. Maybe they're farther away."

What if someone asked why she and Mom didn't visit Dad's grave? What would she say? That they had left him and the house and everything that reminded them of him? But that, in spite of everything, he was always present?

Mom opened the first folder, and math problems, solved and unsolved, leaped off the top paper. Relief flooded Isabelle. Mom was doing something normal, not staring. In gratitude, she walked to Mom and kissed her check. Mom smiled. That was a good sign.

"See you later," she said, turning to leave. She would knock on Margaret's door. Maybe her brain would freeze on the way over and, with it, her memory.

16

BACKBONE ENGAGED

Isabelle began to count the days until Christmas vacation.

"Why do you care about vacation?" Grace demanded as the girls walked back to school after lunch. "Isn't that just more time for you to spend with Miss Flora?"

"Grace, that's mean," said Margaret. "It's nice of Isabelle to visit Miss Flora while her sister is gone."

"How is her sister, anyway?"

"I guess she's getting better although my mom says that's pretty unusual. She says it's a miracle that pneumonia hasn't taken her yet." Isabelle paused. "When can we go shopping downtown? And bake Christmas cookies?"

"Anytime," said Margaret.

"Bake at your house?"

"Maybe. But it can be hard with the twins around. They want to make their own cookies and feed cookie dough to their dolls and put sprinkles in their hair and everything."

"I don't mind," said Isabelle. Margaret's house vibrated with activity. She was part of a pack there.

"We could go to your house," Grace said to Isabelle.

"Maybe." She didn't want to bake at her house. Mom would act cheerful, which was almost worse than looking as if she needed a shot of adrenaline.

The girls ran up the staircase to the third floor, hung up their jackets, and slid into their seats. Their classmates raced in behind them.

The bell rang. Sister Mary Mercy rose from the chair behind her desk, walked to the room's front door and pulled it shut, and scurried to the back door and slammed it. The kids who arrived late opened the doors and slunk to their seats.

With most of the criminals in their places, Sister glared at the class. "Time and again I have beseeched you to return from lunch promptly and in a spirit of readiness to learn. This class has tested me mightily. Beginning tomorrow, we will institute a policy of intolerance toward those who do not respect the time of others."

Sister scoured the room with her eyes, dark points that detected each student's character flaws. "I am seeking a captain to monitor the door after lunch. That person will lock the door as the bell rings. The transgressors—those who arrive after the bell has sounded—will be dealt with by me after school," she said. "Actually, two captains will be chosen, one for each door."

Before dropping her eyes and hoping to shrink, Isabelle glanced at Grace. Grace raised her eyebrows and smiled knowingly; she would not be chosen.

Sister surveyed the saints and sinners of Room 316. Isabelle imagined that she was tallying the virtues and failings of each according to her personal code of behavior as adapted from the New Testament.

Sister's eyes rested on her. Not this, please, Isabelle prayed. Not the job of monitor, a tiny police force. She could almost feel the pressure of Sister's hand on her head, an anointing.

"You will each write your name on a slip of paper neatly torn from your tablet," Sister commanded. "There will be a drawing, a fair competition. However, if a captain is late to his or her post, there will be dire consequences."

Isabelle relaxed. A favorite student wouldn't be chosen. But what if her name was drawn? She folded the bottom of a piece of notebook paper, creased it with her fingernail, and carefully pulled the strip off. With three kids out sick, Isabelle had a one-in-twenty-five chance of being one of the two chosen.

Those were good odds, but not foolproof. She hurriedly printed "Mark Martino" on the paper, folded it, and passed it to the front of the row.

Sister collected the papers in an old shoebox that she kept in her metal cupboard. Then, without fanfare, she picked one piece of paper and unfolded it. "Mark Martino," she said, "will be the keeper of the keys at the front door." A team player, Mark looked pleased. Sister unfolded a second paper. "Linda McGarvey," she announced, "will monitor the back door with our second set of classroom keys." Linda gave Sister a slight nod of acknowledgment. "Just in case one of you is absent, I'll choose an alternate," Sister said, opening a third paper. "Mark Martino," she read, looking quizzically at the name.

A buzz rose from the desks.

Now alert to the subterfuge, Sister demanded, "Who, yes, *who* used Mark's name rather than his own?"

Silence prevailed. Isabelle's brain stopped working.

"*Who* failed to write his own name?"

Would Sister rip out their fingernails in an attempt to find the truth? Bring in a handwriting expert? Somehow, Isabelle knew that she would be martyred, whether in a group or individually. Either way, she would be found out. She didn't have the will to resist her fate.

Her arm was the heaviest thing she had ever

lifted, but, in order to prevent an inquisition, she raised it. She was weary of everything: trying to wriggle away from a job as the Room 316 police force, a new house that wasn't her house, a cemetery with gates that locked behind you, a new school where you had to learn which kids were creepy, landladies to whom death clung, the loss of a dad who loved her without reservation.

Sister stared without speaking.

"Sister, I can't take that job," Isabelle said.

Sister continued to stare.

"I don't mean to be disrespectful, but I can't do it."

Sister looked as if she had been slapped. Her arm levitated to shoulder height, and her pointer finger directed Isabelle to the door. "You will now march," she said, enunciating every syllable, "to the office."

Without meaning to mimic the cadence of Sister's voice, Isabelle asked, "What will I do, when I arrive?"

The class erupted in laughter.

"Silence!" Sister roared. Her finger repeatedly stabbed the air in Isabelle's direction. "To . . . the . . . OFFICE!"

Isabelle stood slowly. What could the principal do? Expel her? She looked at Margaret, who almost shone with awe and dread.

What would Dad think? When she was little, Isabelle sat on the edge of the bathtub while he shaved.

Dad would listen or talk even as he shaved the strip above his top lip. Now the spicy shaving cream filled the inside of Isabelle's head, comforting and familiar. It foamed around her in pure-white whipped swirls. The foam kept building, cool and smooth. Isabelle walked through it, a sea of shaving cream that parted like the Red Sea for Moses, past the hot breath of Charles Hager and the body odor of Ralph Longstreet, as she slogged down the stairs to the principal's office.

17

A LITTLE LESS SORROW

"They called your mom?" Grace repeated to Isabelle in disbelief.

"She made it in fifteen minutes," Isabelle answered. "The assistant principal at her school had to take her class."

"I can't believe they made her talk to Sister Ann Marie for such a stupid thing," said Grace.

The girls walked slowly, savoring every scrap of the scene in the office.

"I've never heard of a parent coming to school except for a conference or book fair," Margaret said.

"And your mom wasn't mad at you?" Grace said.

"Not at me, no. She said that kind of job should be voluntary and that I must have felt pressured to be in the lottery."

"Not even a little mad?"

"She was calm. On the way out, she told me that dumb little things aren't worth making a fuss over."

"Was Sister Ann Marie mad?" Margaret said.

"No, she's really nice. She just asked me why I did it, and I told her."

"But you had kind of lied to a nun," said Grace.

"I guess I did. So I was punished."

"Big punishment," Grace said, as she turned left on Harriet Avenue. "See you tomorrow."

When Grace was out of earshot, Isabelle asked Margaret, "Does her mother stand up for her?"

"It's hard to describe. You could say that her mother hardly stands up."

"Is something wrong with her?" Isabelle pulled up the hood of her jacket.

"Not that you can see. She doesn't like to get out of her bed very much."

"Is she sick?"

"She seems, well, lazy. Grace watches the little kids more than her mom does. She makes dinner, too, unless her dad gets home early. It's been that way since I met Grace."

"Is Grace as happy as she acts?"

"She's just Grace. She's happy most of the time, excited about things, really. But once in a while she's down."

Isabelle wanted to ask, Do you think she resents me for moving across the street from you and being at your house a lot? She didn't.

A soft snowball hit Isabelle in the back. She turned to see Margaret's brother, Mark, running across the street with his friends.

"He just wants your attention," Margaret said.

"I know."

"I think he has a crush on you. Grace likes you, too. I know she does."

Isabelle wanted to ask Margaret if she was happy to have her living across the street. Margaret called a lot and invited her over. But did Grace really like her? Grace wouldn't have sounded the mouse alert for just anyone, would she?

A park police car drove past the girls in the direction of the cemetery. "I wonder if that's Officer Ryan," Isabelle said. "It was awful to be locked in the cemetery. But he was nice, I guess."

"What's happening with Miss Dora?" said Margaret.

"She's in a nursing home now. No one knows if she'll ever come home. If she doesn't, things won't be balanced."

"Balanced?"

"Miss Flora needs her. She likes to take care of people. Even if Miss Dora seems independent, she's still someone for Miss Flora to flutter over."

"Flutter?"

"Like a mother hen, maybe. That's why she likes having us there, I think. Maybe she imagines that

I'm one of her daughters. She told my mom about her own kids. I'll tell you about them."

Between the paint store and the park, Isabelle told Margaret about Mary Catherine, Helen, Alice, and Dora.

"It's terrible," said Margaret. "I wish you hadn't told me the part about the little girls lined up at the window."

"I'm sorry."

"No, it's good that you did. Otherwise you'd be carrying it around by yourself."

Mom had told her, and now she had told Margaret. Could you dilute your sadness by sharing it? Would it be like letting just a little pressure out of a balloon?

"Do you want to make snow cones tonight after we do our homework?" Isabelle said. "There's almost enough snow. We have maple syrup."

"Sure. We'll celebrate. You stood up for yourself. Nobody in our room does that."

"What about Charles Hager?"

"He doesn't really stand up for himself because nobody expects anything of him."

"I'll see you later," Isabelle said as she crossed the street to the duplex. What a relief to know that she wouldn't be the class jailer. What a relief to know that Margaret lived across the street.

18

"CLAIR DE LUNE"

When she opened the door to the duplex, Isabelle heard soft music broken by a smattering of scratchy patches on the record that played in the McCarthys' living room. She pictured Miss Flora behind the door to her living room, alone among the doilies. She knocked.

"It's open. Come in."

Isabelle turned the doorknob and pushed the door slowly as if excessive force might topple an upright Miss Flora. But Miss Flora sat in an armchair, hands clasped in her lap.

"How dear of you to pay me a visit, Little Isabelle," she said.

"I heard the music. It's so sad."

"Why, it's 'Clair de Lune.' Have you never heard it? Mr. Debussy wrote it." Miss Flora spoke of the composer as if they were old friends. She reached into her sweater pocket, pulled out her compact, and powdered her nose as if preparing for Mr. Debussy to walk through the door.

"How can you stand it? I've only heard a little bit, and I want to cry."

"Oh, Little Isabelle." Miss Flora giggled. "You caught me unaware. I'm just sitting here having one of my sad moments, and you come along and lift me out of myself."

"You're having a sad moment? Is that like having tea or something?"

Miss Flora laughed appreciatively. "That's simply what I call them. When Dora and I had so much sadness a long time ago, I didn't think we would recover. I was drooping away from life, you might say."

"That's hard to imagine." Isabelle lowered herself on the couch. She was sure she smelled brownies.

"You didn't know me then, dear. I used to stay in my nightgown all day sometimes. I was so sad that I couldn't see that my husband and Dora were sad, too." Miss Flora looked startled, as if she had forgotten that Isabelle was sitting only inches away. "I'm sorry to be going on like this."

"My mom told me about your children."

"She did?" Miss Flora relaxed into the armchair. "Long ago, Dora came home with some lovely music by Mr. Debussy—and she played it on the Victrola until it seemed I had used up a lifetime's supply of tears."

"Because of the music?"

"Yes, because the music found a little crack in me, and it dug into the hard knot of sorrow that had grown inside. I told myself, 'You have been hurt beyond measure.' Very gradually, I tried to work a little or care about someone else. I knew that I could always return to my sad moments, but I wouldn't stay in them."

Miss Flora had never made such a long speech about anything. Isabelle answered with a respectful silence because Miss Flora appeared lost in the melody.

When the song ended, Isabelle asked, "Do you need a record player when you want to be in a sad moment?"

"Dear Isabelle, you know that I don't need a record player to ponder sorrow," she said, wagging her finger playfully. "But I do need my music sometimes. It's as if someone is sharing his or her sorrow with me. Then I acknowledge mine. Sometimes I give myself over when I see a beautiful picture or read a lovely passage in a book. I give in to the sadness, but I know I will go on. Would you like a brownie?"

Mom sat in a chair at the kitchen table, her fingers wrapped around a cup of tea. She stared out the window that was fogged with steam from the kettle.

Slowly she turned to Isabelle and said, "I heard you downstairs. I've been waiting to find out how you are after what happened at school."

"I'm fine," said Isabelle, setting a plate of brownies on the table. "Thanks for rescuing me."

"You know that I only put in an appearance because it was expected. The whole thing was so ridiculous. It's not as if you were cheating on a test."

Mom's words were worrisome. As a teacher, she didn't criticize other teachers. She didn't condone lying, either, if that's what Isabelle had done.

"I wish that I could tell your father about it," Mom said.

"Your father." How many times had they mentioned him out loud since he'd been gone? Once? Twice? Dad dictated their lives, but talking about him was as jarring as a jackhammer going off in the living room.

"We should have stayed in our house," Mom said, looking at Isabelle briefly before returning her gaze to the window, covered with slop that looked like melting sky. "You had Carol and your other friends. But I couldn't bear being in the house or even looking in the mirror he used. I didn't want to see myself there." She shook her head as if trying to clear it. "I called Carol's mother after I came home today. If you want, you can stay with Carol's family as long as you like. They would love to have you."

The earth cracked open. Mom wanted her to leave? "You want me to go?" Isabelle said.

"No. But you might be happier there."

"But I'm here now."

"Do you want to be here? That's what I'm asking."

"I want to be in our old house. I want everything to be the way it was."

Resting her forearms on her thighs, Mom put her face in her hands and cried softly. Isabelle felt as helpless as if Mom were under ice on a lake. Would this be the time to borrow Miss Flora's record?

"No more changes," Isabelle said. "Look, Miss Flora sent brownies. Let's have one. Here. Look." She swallowed hard. "Dad would want us to have a brownie."

Downstairs, Miss Flora's music played on.

19
AN UNWRAPPABLE GIFT

On the following Saturday, Isabelle stayed in bed until she couldn't sleep anymore. Then she picked *Little Women* off the floor and started reading. A few seconds after the phone rang, Mom tapped on her door. "Isabelle, it's Margaret."

"What time is it?"

"Almost twelve thirty."

"Here I come." The floor was cold, but the kitchen was warm and fragrant with baking bread. The telephone receiver seemed to smell of yeast. Mom had the will to rise and pummel dough, a habit she hadn't resumed until now.

"Hi," Isabelle said to Margaret. "What's up?"

"I need to get out of here. I'm done vacuuming, and my mom said that I can go downtown. Can you come?"

"I think so. When?"

"As soon as you get here," said Margaret. "Then I'll call Grace and tell her we're ready. She gets on any number 4 bus, and we watch for the one she's on."

"How do you know she's on it?"

"She sits in front and smashes her face into the window so we know it's the right one."

"Okay. I just have to get dressed." The snow outside the window descended slowly, as if it were a warm-up act for a serious snowfall. "Do I need to bring anything?"

"Just money for a slice of pizza or a record or presents if you're shopping and bus fare."

After Isabelle hung up the phone, she watched Mom shape dough into a loaf. "I'm going downtown," she said. "Is that okay?"

"Sure. Take some money out of my purse so that I don't have to wash my hands," said Mom.

In Milwaukee, Isabelle babysat for two families, the O'Connors—with their grinning, bouncing baby, Thomas—and the Hood kids. Ten-year-old Martin Hood stood out; he once asked Isabelle to proofread his letter to Queen Elizabeth II. Now cut off from babysitting revenue, Isabelle relied on Mom for a small allowance.

Mom's hands continued to work independently of her thoughts. "I know you'll have fun," she said.

"Are you having fun?" Isabelle asked, realizing that she rarely asked Mom anything for fear of the answer.

"It's good to have something to do on weekends," she said, forming another loaf. "And I'm going to see Cindy after I visit Dora."

Dad had always demanded a crust as soon as the bread came out of the oven. Isabelle imagined waiting for the timer to go off and then asking Mom for a crust. But she didn't.

The radio announcer's voice filled the pause in conversation, and Isabelle realized that until today Mom hadn't turned the kitchen radio on. In Milwaukee it was always on—at least in the morning—for news and weather and music.

"Have fun with Cindy," Isabelle said. "Say hi to Miss Dora."

Looking like a flattened alien, Grace pressed her face against the bus window so that Isabelle and Margaret knew they were boarding the right bus. The walk from the bus was chilling, but the girls paused at the department store window that showcased Santa's workshop.

"I've never been this cold under such a blue sky," Margaret said, shivering.

"How could you forget what January is like?" said Grace. "Brace yourself, Isabelle. Now look at the size of that giraffe. How did they get *that* here from the North Pole?"

"Santa must have sent elves to assemble it," said Isabelle. "Can you believe all of it?" She lingered on the animals and dolls and toys that made her want to crawl into the window and be a part of such delight.

The sidewalk teemed with people—cheeks pink with cold, scarves flapping in the wind—who carried shopping bags bearing department store names. Cars crawled along Nicollet Avenue, passengers staring at the holiday windows. Salvation Army bell ringers played the familiar melody—da *ding*, da *ding*, da *ding*—that promised a Merry Christmas for all if you could only spare some change today. At Christmastime last year, Isabelle and Mom and Dad had gone as usual to see the Christmas tree at City Hall in Milwaukee.

"This way!" Grace called. "Cinderella's ball in the window. They're dancing."

"I'm freezing," Margaret said. "Let's stop on the way out."

"Is this where we're going?" Isabelle asked. She opened the department store door. Christmas carols rose above the din of shoppers' voices. As the girls moved toward the bank of elevators, fragrances greeted them: perfume samples on wrists, leather belts and purses hanging from pegs, gingerbread men that beckoned from the bakery.

One by one, they stepped off the elevator, and Isabelle followed Margaret and Grace to the record department where Bing Crosby filled the air with "I'll Be Home for Christmas."

"I don't know why my mom is so crazy about him," Grace said.

"I'd rather listen to him than Alvin and the Chipmunks and their Christmas noise," said Margaret.

Even though everything was familiar—the music, the record displays, the bustle—suddenly Isabelle felt out of place, drowning, almost. Last year, she had Carol and the others. This year, she clung to Margaret.

Are you my friend? Or do you feel sorry for me? Again she desperately wanted to ask Margaret. Her need for reassurance consumed her to the point of panic. If she asked Margaret, Margaret would tell her what she wanted to hear. She was too nice to do otherwise.

Grace stood in a row of record bins, flipping through the Ms. "Margaret," she called. "You want 'Moon River,' right?"

Isabelle didn't know what Margaret wanted. "Are you okay?" Margaret said. "You look a little lost."

"I'm okay."

"Christmas is probably really hard for you."

Isabelle didn't answer. Last year she had given Dad an album of organ music that he liked.

"We'll bake cookies tomorrow at my house," Margaret said. "In the afternoon. We'll walk to the store later today to get anything special that we need."

"Okay."

"What are you talking about?" Grace called. "Are you conspiring against me?"

"Of course," Margaret said. "What else would we talk about?"

Margaret turned back to Isabelle. "We'll make a thousand cookies."

"I heard that," Grace said. "What about me?"

"Of course you can come," said Margaret. "It's a friends-only party."

Isabelle's heart calmed. She relaxed. These must be her friends, she hoped.

20

SPEAKING THE UNSPEAKABLE

Isabelle woke to a driving wet slop that pelted the house. She pulled the covers over her head. Another Saturday, and the sky could cry all the big tears it wanted. She didn't have to get up and go out in it and be soaked before she got to school. A soft line of light reached under the door. She listened. Why wasn't the radio on? Why wasn't Mom punching down bread dough or loudly slaying vegetables for soup with what Dad called "the farmer's wife's carving knife"? Why wasn't Miss Flora running water for oatmeal or her African violets' breakfast downstairs?

With the floor creaking in protest, Isabelle padded to the door and opened it a crack. The lamp in the living room beamed at her. Mom wasn't there or in the dining room. In the kitchen, breadcrumbs waited on the cutting board, advertising breaded pork chops for supper. The back door stood open, so Isabelle tip-toed down the stairs to the McCarthy kitchen. Miss Flora's soft sobs were overlaid with Mom's murmurs.

Could Miss Dora have died? Why else would the breadcrumbs be abandoned and tears flowing? Isabelle climbed back up the steps as quietly as she could. In her room, she dressed quickly. Her only thought: get away.

As she took her jacket from the coat closet, she saw the black umbrella leaning upright in the corner, the same position it had held in the closet in Milwaukee. Isabelle considered it, glanced outside, and left it. The slop had stopped raining down. As an after-thought, she went to her room and ripped a sheet of paper from a tablet.

"Went for a walk," she wrote. No need to sign it—I'm the only one here, she thought.

Milwaukee was east, so that was the direction she chose. She passed Lyndale Farmstead Park as she did almost every day. Margaret had said that it actually was a farm when some of her aunts and uncles were children. Who cared? She walked past Mom's school, Agassiz, and then hers; the building looked grim and embarrassed for Isabelle, treading there on a Saturday. Across the street stood the church, spire tall and grave. Would Miss Dora's funeral be there?

Dad's funeral Mass had not been said at the par-ish church. His service took place at a mortuary with hotel lobby furnishings and folding chairs. In spite of the sanctions placed on the burial because of the circumstances of Dad's death, Father Cleary had spoken at the mortuary and ridden to the cemetery with Isabelle and Mom.

Isabelle walked through neighborhoods dotted with corner grocery stores and drugstores, barbershops and taverns. She walked past the Riverview Theater and another public school, Howe. After what seemed like hours, she came to the river, wide and visible because the tree branches had lost their leaves. The sky began to leak a misty insult, and Isabelle sat on a wet bench and stared at the mighty Mississippi below.

Miss Dora's funeral would be sad. Would she miss Miss Dora? Miss Dora had reminded Miss Flora that Isabelle had a name besides "Little Girl." She had tried to fill her with oatmeal. She had borne the loss of a husband and little nieces. A million years ago, she had been young.

But could she ever mourn anyone except for Dad, so full of life?

"Why are you crying?" Out of nowhere, a little boy materialized next to the bench. His mother pushed a tricycle on the sidewalk. Isabelle wiped her eyes on her coat sleeve and wished the boy would disappear.

"Johnny," the woman called. "Get back on your trike."

"Why are you crying?" the little boy repeated. His

mother approached, now carrying her son's tricycle over the dead grass. "She's crying," the boy said.

Looking concerned, the woman asked, "Is there anything we can do for you?"

"No," said Isabelle, fumbling in her pocket for a handkerchief.

"Are you sure?"

Isabelle nodded.

"All right." Johnny's mother pointed across the street, and Isabelle's eyes followed. "But if you need anything, we live in the fourth house from the corner, right there. If you want to use our phone or anything."

Johnny climbed on his trike and struggled to pedal over the sodden ground. He chattered to his mother as the sleet ramped up and slid down their yellow slickers.

The dampness seeped through Isabelle's corduroy pants to her skin. What a long walk back it would be, she thought, not really caring. Her mind felt as cold as her feet and her backside.

She stood, turned from the river, and walked. A police car glided by and, for a moment, she imagined that Officer Ryan drove it, sent to rescue her. The window went down and an arm waved through the curtain of sleet. Isabelle squinted at a gray-haired officer. Her feet squished inside her loafers.

In the distance, two figures approached, bobbing under umbrellas. In Milwaukee, Isabelle and Carol had taken "nowhere walks" in all weather. They never ran out of things to say to each other.

Snow and slop took turns dripping out of the sky, unsure as to the preferred method of drowning Isabelle. She slogged across another street, not bothering to avoid puddles as she and the advancing umbrellas moved closer to each other, now on the same block. Walk between those carefree girls, Isabelle told herself. Split those two bouncing along, yellow umbrella and red umbrella mocking the gray sky. Could she do it?

An arm shot out from beneath the yellow umbrella, waving. Isabelle peered at the approaching hooded heads. "Isabelle," a voice called, "couldn't you ford the river?"

"We can call my dad," said the other, "if you're as wet as we are. There's a phone booth back there." Margaret and Grace—looking solid, purposeful, and soggy—stood in front of Isabelle.

"My dad saw you from the barbershop," Margaret said. "We hoped that you were going in a straight line so that we could find you. I thought you might like company."

"I'm the backup company," said Grace.

"Miss Dora died," said Isabelle. Margaret and Grace exchanged a confused look.

"Miss Dora? I saw Miss Flora waiting for a cab," Margaret said. "She asked why you weren't with us."

"But she was crying this morning."

"She was probably crying because Miss Dora is still in that nursing home. I think we would know if she'd died," Margaret reasoned. "I'm pretty sure she didn't die."

Isabelle watched the water run over the curb. The words in her wanted to escape, and she tried to stop them. But they slipped out, without permission. "My dad died," she said.

Margaret and Grace waited, water slipping off their umbrellas.

"Except that he didn't just die. He killed himself. In our house. I found him. My mom slapped me in the face to keep me away."

No one spoke. Margaret and Grace looked as if they had been slapped. Isabelle wanted to say, no, it's not true.

Margaret picked up Isabelle's hand, hidden in a soggy mitten.

"If anything bad had happened to me, it would have killed my dad," Isabelle said, softly crying the words out. "He was perfect. He taught me how to score a baseball card when I was seven. He made up a story with me in it almost every night. He made everything fun."

Margaret gently pulled Isabelle between her and Grace.

"I love him more than anyone." Isabelle couldn't tell if rain or tears streamed down her face. "I don't know why he would do that to us." She gulped as she cried.

Margaret opened her mouth to speak, but Isabelle stopped her. "Don't say that I'll be okay," she said. "Please. Don't say that time will help."

No one said anything. They began to walk, Margaret and Grace making a canopy with their umbrellas, covering Isabelle in the middle.

21

LIGHT UP

On the way to school, Isabelle could hardly believe that every snowflake was unique, even though she knew it was. She saw patterns, but within each flake the details varied. Sometimes one snowflake collided with another, creating a new design. She thought of Margaret, who walked with her, and Grace, who would join them. They had linked together to create a new design themselves. A safe place.

With Christmas vacation looming, Sister Mary Mercy's class sent out a low, electric buzz of anticipation. Sister did not suppress it. Sometimes, before the holidays, she abandoned some of her more severe practices. Since no one had been late for five days in a row, the after-lunch monitors had been temporarily retired. A spelling bee with words related to Advent and Christmas replaced an entire religion class.

One morning, Sister stopped Isabelle at the door. "Isabelle," she said, "you are an asset to our class."

Isabelle wasn't sure of the correct response, so she said, "Thank you, Sister."

"I apologize if I was unduly harsh with you recently."

Isabelle reeled. Who had ever heard of a nun apologizing to a student?

"But I may have an opportunity that you'll enjoy very soon," Sister continued. "I'm planning a little experiment, you might say."

"Oh," was the only sound that Isabelle could form as she opened the door for Sister and followed her into the room.

On the way home for lunch, Isabelle told Margaret and Grace about the brief encounter.

"Maybe she's trying to get you to sign up to be a nun," Grace said. "We might be almost old enough."

"Maybe she just likes you," said Margaret. "She never turned on you after that door monitor flop."

The day before Christmas vacation began, Charles Hager drove to school in a 1956 Oldsmobile. He parked behind the building, snug against the gym windows. Mary Ann Murray, who was looking out the window as she watered the ivy in the St. Therese the Little Flower planter, spread the word. Isabelle and other kids raced to look at Charles, who smoked as he leaned against the car.

"He must be older than we are," Isabelle said to Margaret.

"Charles might know how to drive, but he couldn't have a license. He was only one grade ahead of me when I started first grade."

"Look at this!" screamed Peter Janicek. "Sister is in the alley!"

With her back to the class, Sister was engaged in conversation with Charles. It was odd to see a nun outside the building unless she was briskly crossing the street to the convent. Sister and Charles moved along the school in the direction of the side door. By the time they had climbed the stairs, every student in Room 316—except for Charles—tingled in his or her seat in anticipation of an unimaginable scene.

Charles followed Sister into the room. As usual, his brown uniform shirt was not tucked into his pants, which were not the required tweed uniform slacks.

After morning prayers, the Pledge of Allegiance, attendance, and a notice read about the Christmas Day Mass schedule, the class seemed to slump, sensing that Charles and his car would not be an immediate distraction.

But Sister did not disappoint. "Although I am not your science teacher," she said, "Charles has agreed to help me carry out a brief experiment. And I believe that Isabelle will help me, too."

So this was her reward, a science experiment with Charles.

"First, I'm going to ask Charles a question," Sister continued. "Charles, for how long have you smoked cigarettes?"

Charles smiled sheepishly. "Since the summer before sixth grade."

"Charles, please walk up and down the aisles with your palms up, allowing your classmates to inspect your fingers."

Ralph Longstreet gave Charles the kind of grin you would give your buddy for tripping a fourth-grader.

Everyone knew that Charles's fingers were a sickening color, rusted yellow. As he wove through the aisles, he savored the attention even though the comments were predictable, a weak "yuck" or "smell as bad as they look."

"Isabelle, please come to the front of the room."

Isabelle could almost feel Margaret's heart sink with her own. Was she too weak to protest or was she getting used to standing in front of the room to read her book reports? She knew all the faces now—they weren't a blur anymore—and most of the kids were nice enough. She rose from her seat and took her place next to Sister.

Sister smiled at Isabelle, then turned to Charles and spoke. "Charles, even though you know what cigarettes have done to your fingers, and the surgeon general of our country has told us that smoking may do serious damage to your lungs, why do you continue to smoke?"

Grinning broadly, Charles faced the class. "I smoke," he said, "because it's cool."

Snickers erupted.

"All right, then, Charles. Please light a cigarette for Isabelle."

Wasn't this against the law? A model student forced to smoke? Margaret looked stricken, and Grace's eyes looked about to blow out of her face. The lighter made a *whoosh* as Charles lit the cigarette held in the corner of his mouth.

"Here, Isabelle." Charles, who had never spoken to her before, handed her a lit Camel, unfiltered.

"Just a little puff," said Sister. "Don't try to inhale. See how the smoke tastes."

Where was Mom when she needed her? Isabelle looked at Margaret, who looked as if she had just used a knife to remove toast from a plugged-in toaster. The class stared in shocked silence.

Suddenly something cracked inside Isabelle. She felt like a soft-boiled egg when the spoon hits. Her yolk was running. She had made Dad laugh every day of his life except for the days she tried to forget. Where had that Isabelle gone?

She knew that Sister expected her to go down coughing or gagging, a live antismoking poster.

Without preamble, Isabelle sucked slowly and cautiously on the cigarette and puffed her cheeks out, holding the smoke without inhaling. Then, lips tight, she blew it out her nose in a stream like Grandpa did, a dragon blowing fire. The smoke rose a little, and Isabelle blinked it away.

"Well!" Sister said, looking amazed.

All eyes were glued to Isabelle. "Very, very . . . tasty!" she said.

Shrieks of laughter shot out like screams. Martin Green stood, held his stomach, and cried, "Make it stop hurting!" before he collapsed on his desktop. Margaret laughed until tears ran down her face. Grace's head was down, and she pounded the desk with one hand.

Isabelle stood still until the noise was a murmur. She looked at Sister, who now held Charles's cigarette in one hand. Leaning on the blackboard with one arm bent, Sister lifted the cigarette to her mouth and sucked on it as if it promised eternal salvation. She tipped her head back and blew smoke toward the ceiling.

For a second time, the class erupted, slowly at first, then with a roar. Sister continued to draw on the cigarette, blowing smoke toward the class as she strode back and forth, her rosary beads exclaiming.

"This is *not* cool," she said to Charles when she stopped. "You don't look different from any other smoker. It will kill you. If I could quit, you can." She coughed deeply. "Besides, it's nasty."

"Thank you," she said to Isabelle. "I knew I'd find the right volunteer project for you."

I love it, Isabelle said to herself. I love to make people laugh. I do.

That evening, as Kathleen and Karen brushed their dolls' hair at the dining room table, Isabelle sat in Margaret's kitchen with Margaret and Grace.

"Talk louder!" Kathleen commanded. "Or we'll have to bring all the barrettes in there so we can hear you."

"Do it again, Isabelle," Grace pleaded. "Imitate yourself. Then Sister."

"Let her rest," said Margaret. "She's done it a hundred times."

"But it's so good."

"I still can't believe I did it," said Isabelle.

"Sister must have wanted you to choke so that no one would ever light up," Grace said. "Can you believe she ever smoked? She was probably born before cigarettes were invented."

Carrying a full basket of clean laundry, Margaret's mother emerged from the basement. "Sister Mary Mercy? She's not that old."

"About five hundred years?" said Grace. "Or older. I think that tobacco was here before Columbus."

"Maybe sixty?" Margaret's mother guessed.

"Maybe what they say about cigarettes wrecking your insides goes for the outside, too," said Margaret.

"Are you smiling because you're funny?" Grace asked Isabelle.

"No," Isabelle said. "I'm smiling because I can imagine my dad laughing." It hurt to know that she could never tell him. But she had told Mom. Mom was awed.

22
SNOW ANGELS

On Sunday morning, Isabelle and Mom walked home from church.

Officer Ryan had sat with them, asking if it was okay as he genuflected at the end of the pew.

"Would you like a ride home?" he said after Mass.

"Maybe another time," said Mom. "I like to stretch my legs."

"I'll see you around," he said. Without his uniform, he looked even younger.

When he was out of earshot, Isabelle said, "I think he has a crush on you."

"He can have a crush on me," said Mom. "I don't mind. But remember, my heart belongs to Timmy Staples."

"Still?"

"At least until the end of this subbing job. He's such a dear little kid."

The sun made a brief yet timid appearance.

"Mom?" Isabelle said.

"Yes?"

"Dad was perfect, wasn't he?"

Mom didn't look at her as she walked. "He was." She raised her chin a little. "He was perfect, and he was perfectly wonderful."

Isabelle shut her eyes for a moment and felt the sun on her lids. She saw Dad with the crinkles that erupted around his eyes when he smiled as he zoomed into a room to pick both her and Mom up at the same time. "He really liked you," Isabelle said. "I mean, he loved you."

Mom took Isabelle's hand and held it as if Isabelle were pulling away. Isabelle held on. "I know," Mom said. "And you. He loved you so much." She continued walking without releasing Isabelle's hand. "I want him back so much sometimes that I can hardly bear it. Even knowing the hard times. But I have you. And what do you have?"

Photos? Isabelle thought. Books he read to me? The dresser he had when he was a boy? None of those things really mattered. Only Dad mattered.

"I have you," she echoed Mom as neither let go of the other's hand. Mom would want to hear that. "And my friends. I have the good things that happened, and the good things that haven't happened yet." Mom would like to hear that, too. Maybe it would be true a long time from now.

Mom nodded solemnly. "Will you talk to me sometimes?" she said. "About Dad. About us. It's so quiet in our house."

"Sure," Isabelle said. She couldn't handle too much talking with Mom yet. But they were talking now, weren't they? It was okay. It wasn't killing anyone.

They let go of each other's hand. Isabelle slipped her arm through Mom's arm as they walked.

Miss Flora had invited Isabelle and Mom to breakfast. She placed a golden waffle in front of each of them and plopped a dollop of soft butter on top. From the stove she carried a pan of steaming water from which a bottle of maple syrup rose, reminding Isabelle of a little prairie dog peeking out of its hole.

"Oh, the milk!" Miss Flora exclaimed.

"I'll get it," said Isabelle. The inside of the refrigerator looked like a museum of old-people's food: plumped prunes, buttermilk, orange marmalade, and cottage cheese. Isabelle reached for the quart bottle.

"Drink all you want, Isabelle," Miss Flora said as Isabelle poured. "The milkman comes tomorrow. How is school going for you?" she asked between tiny bites of waffle.

"Not bad. We're on vacation now. Sister seemed happy about that."

"And Margaret and her friend Grace, will you see them during vacation?"

"Sure."

"I mostly see Grace in the nice weather when she's flying by on her bike. She seems such a spirited girl."

"She's smart in school," said Isabelle, "and a little bossy, but very nice. She likes to have the last word. She doesn't care what people think of her as much as some kids do."

"Maybe she doesn't care," Miss Flora said. "Or maybe she does, and it's easy for her to pretend she doesn't." Miss Flora paused as if picturing Grace tearing down the street on her bike. "And Margaret is a good friend, isn't she? I see you going off on all sorts of adventures."

"Margaret is . . . Margaret." She was so many things. Isabelle picked one. "She's steadfast."

"Steadfast! That's a wonderful word from my day!" said Miss Flora. "And what are you in this trio, Isabelle?"

"I'm Isabelle Day of Milwaukee."

"You're so much more," Miss Flora said. "I would say you're a lifesaver."

By late afternoon, snow was falling so furiously that Miss Flora called her daughter in St. Paul and told her to cancel the visit to Miss Dora. Isabelle poked her head into the lower duplex on her way outside to shovel.

"Come in!" Miss Flora said. She held a framed black-and-white photograph of her four oldest daughters in front of a house. "This fell off the wall yesterday," she said. "It's good for me to stop and take a long, close look at my little girls. I never want to forget how much I loved them."

Isabelle put her hand out for the photograph. The girls were beautiful, the two older ones with loopy curls made, she knew, by setting hair with strips of cloth. The third-tallest girl had a hair bow that peeked out from behind her head and a smile almost as wide. The little one, Dora, broadcast mischief.

"She was just like my sister," Miss Flora said, pointing.

Isabelle remained silent. How could she respond? "The girls are so pretty," she said.

"They will always be my four little girls," said Miss Flora, "even though they're not here." She smiled as she put her handkerchief in the sleeve of her sweater. "And I still keep meeting dear little girls."

After shoveling, Isabelle hung up her coat, put her hat and mittens on the radiator, and changed into dry socks. She sat at the kitchen table reading the Sunday comics as Mom peeled potatoes for dinner.

Someone knocked at the door, and Isabelle ran to answer it. "Mom, there are snow angels here," she called back to the kitchen.

Margaret and Grace stepped into the living room. Snow topped their hats and shoulders and coated their jackets. Their eyelashes were as white as the frosted hair that framed their faces.

"We decided to see what you're up to," Grace said.

"Yes, you're angels," Mom said, looking at them. "Beautiful angels, and I wouldn't be one bit surprised to see wings."

"My jackets are always too small," Grace said, turning to show her back. "But my wings are folded up there. Can you see the outline?"

"Why don't you stay here?" said Isabelle. "I just came in. We can play Scrabble." She looked at Mom. "That's what we used to do sometimes on Sunday."

"I'll get the game," Mom said. "Take off your coats, girls, and put them on the radiator. Your hats and mittens, too."

After everyone had settled themselves at the kitchen table, Isabelle picked the highest letter and so went first, making the word "floral."

Grace rubbed her hands together like feelers.

Margaret studied her letters with concern.

Mom put the potatoes in cold water and took cocoa powder from the cupboard.

"This is exactly what I want to be doing right now," Isabelle said. She didn't say that it was her second choice. This was good enough.

During a moment of silence, Miss Flora's grandfather clock chimed four times, just a few seconds before Dad's clock announced the same hour.

Outside, the heavy snowfall had slowed. A lighter snow swirled lazily as if it couldn't decide whether or not to land on the earth. •

ACKNOWLEDGMENTS

I began writing *Isabelle Day Refuses to Die of a Broken Heart* while I was a resident at The Anderson Center for Interdisciplinary Studies in Red Wing, Minnesota. I'm indebted to Robert Hedin and the center's board and staff for the privilege of living and working there.

Kate DiCamillo heard this book first, and her response gave me what I needed to continue. I thank the generous readers Heller Landecker, Phyllis Root, Jane Resh Thomas, and Paula Vandenbosch, as well as every member of every one of my writing groups.

Isabelle Day Refuses to Die of a Broken Heart owes an enormous debt to Graham Gremore, who insisted that I go deeper and also mine any humor that lurked there. His insights, clarity, and dedication to this story guided and uplifted me.

My dear friends Anne Ellingson and Becky Mulen

gave me priceless gifts: Anne saw the snot bubble, and Becky regaled us with tales of Sister Claudina's raucous classroom. Julie Westerberg's trip to the cemetery with an elderly neighbor inspired Isabelle's expedition with the McCarthy sisters. Mary Lou Westerberg, my childhood idol and dear friend, shared her memories of—and her gratitude for—the place where we grew up. My grandmother, Louise Van Braak, wrapped me in love and stories, which I shared with Isabelle.

The Hennepin Medical History Center, Minnesota History Center, and Ann Monson (who spent time in an oxygen tent) helped enormously.

Thank you, Erik Anderson, for bringing this book to light. Because of you, Isabelle Day won't ever die of a broken heart.

Jane St. Anthony grew up in south Minneapolis in a house with a front porch that was perfect for summer reading. She is a freelance writer and leads workshops for young authors. Her two other books for middle-grade readers are *The Summer Sherman Loved Me* and *Grace Above All*, both published by the University of Minnesota Press. She lives in Minneapolis.